PAPER DOLL

Also by Robert B. Parker
in Thorndike Large Print ®

Perchance to Dream
Stardust
Playmates
The Widening Gyre
A Savage Place
Early Autumn
Looking for Rachel Wallace
Promised Land
Mortal Stakes

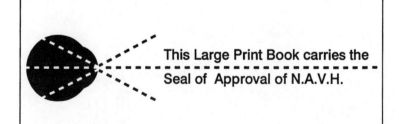

This Large Print Book carries the
Seal of Approval of N.A.V.H.

PAPER DOLL

Robert B. Parker

Thorndike Press • Thorndike, Maine

Thorndike Large Print ® Basic Series edition published in 1993 by arrangement with G.P. Putnam's Sons.

The tree indicium is a trademark of Thorndike Press.

Set in 16 pt. News Plantin by Lynn M. Hathaway.

Printed in the United States on acid-free, high-opacity paper. ⊗

Library of Congress Cataloging in Publication Data

Parker, Robert B., 1932–
    Paper doll / Robert B. Parker.
      p. cm.
    ISBN 0-7862-0003-0 (alk. paper : lg. print)
    ISBN 0-7862-0004-9 (alk. paper : lg. print : pbk)
    1. Large type books. I. Title.
  [PS3566.A686P33 1993b]
  813'.54—dc20   93-22854

For Joan: Music all around me

1

Loudon Tripp, wearing a seersucker suit and a Harvard tie, sat in my office on a very nice day in September and told me he'd looked into my background and might hire me.

"Oh boy," I said.

"You've had some college," Tripp said. He was maybe fifty, a tall angular man with a red face. He held a typewritten sheet of paper in his hand, reading it through half glasses.

"No harm to it," I said. "I thought I was going to do something else."

"I went to Harvard. You played football in college."

I nodded. He didn't care if I nodded or not. But I liked to.

"You were a prizefighter."

Nod.

"You fought in Korea. Were you an officer?"

"No."

"Too bad. After that you were a policeman."

Nod.

"This presents a small problem; you were

dismissed. Could you comment, please, on that."

"I am trustworthy, loyal, and helpful. But I struggle with *obedient*."

Tripp smiled faintly. "I'm not looking for a boy scout," he said.

"Next best thing," I said.

"Well," Tripp said, "Lieutenant Quirk said you could be annoying, but you were not undependable."

"He's always admired me," I said.

"Obviously you are independent," Tripp said. "I understand that. I've had my moments. 'He who would be a man must be a non-conformist.' "

I nodded encouragingly.

"Do you know who said that?" Tripp asked.

I nodded again.

Tripp waited a moment.

Finally he said, "Well, who?"

"Emerson."

"Very good," Tripp said.

"Will this be on the final?" I said.

Tripp leaned his head toward me in a gesture of apology.

"Sorry, I guess that seemed pretentious. It's just that I am trying to get a sense of you."

I shrugged.

"They had no way of judging a man," I said, "except as he handled an axe."

Tripp frowned for a moment. And twitched his shoulders as if to get rid of a horsefly.

"So," he paused. "I guess you'll do."

I tried to look pleased.

He stared past me out the window for a moment, and took in a slow breath and let it out.

"Are you familiar," he said, "with Olivia Nelson?"

"The woman who was murdered a couple of months back," I said. "Right in Louisburg Square."

He nodded.

"She used her birth name," he said. "She was my wife."

"I'm sorry," I said.

"Yes."

We were quiet for a moment while we considered the sullen fact.

"The police have exhausted all of their options," Tripp said. "They have concluded it was probably an act of random violence, and the killer, having left no clues, will very likely not be caught until, or if, he strikes again."

"You disagree?" I said.

"I want him hunted down," Tripp said stiffly, "and punished."

"And you want me to do that?"

"Yes . . . Lieutenant Quirk suggested you,

9

when I expressed concern about the official lack of progress."

"So you and I are clear," I said, "I will hunt him down for you. But punishment is not what I do."

"I believe in the system," Tripp said. "If you can find him, I am sure the courts will punish him."

I said, "Un huh."

"You are skeptical of the courts?" Tripp said.

"I'm skeptical of most things," I said. "Is there anyone assigned to the case, now?"

"Yes, a young detective."

"What's his name?"

"Farrell. Detective Farrell. I can't say I'm entirely happy with him."

"Why?"

"Well, he's young. I was hoping for a more senior man."

I nodded. There was more, I could tell.

"And there's something, a little, I don't know. He doesn't seem like a typical police detective."

I waited. Tripp didn't elaborate. Since I figured I'd meet Farrell anyway, I didn't press. I could decide for myself how typical he was.

"Do you have any theories on the murder?" I said.

"None. I can't imagine who would wish to

kill Olivia. Perhaps it is a madman."

"Okay," I said. "I'll talk to the cops, first. So at least I'll know what they know."

"You'll take the case, then?"

"Sure," I said.

We talked a little about my fee, and the prospects of a retainer. He had no objections to a retainer. Me either.

"The only thing you need to understand," I said, "is that once I start I go where it takes me. Which may mean I ask you lots of questions. And your friends and relatives lots of questions. People sometimes get restive about me invading their privacy. You have to understand at the start that invading your privacy, and the privacy of people you know, is what you're hiring me to do."

"I understand," Tripp said. "If you go too far, I'll let you know."

"You can let me know," I said. "But it won't change anything. I do what I do. And I keep doing it until I'm finished."

"You will be working for me, Mr. Spenser."

"Yes, and you can pay me, and you can expect that I'll work on your problem and that I won't cheat you and that I won't lie to you. But you can't tell me what to do, and if you're not willing to accept that, we can't do business."

Tripp didn't like it. But he got out his

checkbook and put it on the edge of my desk and dug a real fountain pen out of his inside coat pocket.

"When I need surgery," he said, "I don't, I guess, tell the surgeon how to operate."

"Nice analogy," I said.

He nodded, and wrote me out a check in a stately, flowing Palmer-method hand. It was a fine big check. A check you could deposit proudly, which, after Tripp left, I did.

2

"He hit her with a framing hammer," Quirk said. "The kind with the long wooden handle that gives you leverage so you can drive a sixteen-penny nail with two strokes. Hit her at least five times."

Quirk was wearing a gray silk tweed jacket with a faint lavender chalk line, a blue Oxford button-down shirt, and a lavender knit tie. There was a dark blue display handkerchief in his jacket pocket. As he talked, he straightened the stuff on his desk, making sure everything was square and properly spaced. There wasn't much: a phone, a legal-sized lined yellow pad, a translucent Bic pen with a black top, and a big plastic cube with pictures of his wife, his children, and a golden retriever. He was careful to have the cube exactly centered along the back rim of his desk. He wasn't thinking about what he was doing. It was what he did while he thought about something else.

"He left it at the crime scene."

"Or she," I said.

Quirk realigned his pictures an eighth of

13

an inch. His hands were big and thick, the nails manicured. They looked like the hands of a tough surgeon.

"Ah, yes," Quirk said. "Liberation. It could have been a woman. But if it was, it was a strong one. He, or she, must have held the hammer down at the end and taken a full swing, like you would drive a nail. Most of the bones in her head were broken."

"Only the head?"

"Yeah," Quirk said. "That bothered me too. If some fruitcake runs amok with a framing hammer and assaults a random victim, why was his aim so good? Head only. Except where he seems to have missed once and badly bruised her left shoulder."

"Seems more like premeditation," I said. "If you're going to murder somebody with a hammer, you don't waste time hitting them in the body."

"I know," Quirk said. His hands were perfectly still now, one resting on top of the other. "It bothered us too. But things always do in a homicide. You know that. There's always stuff you can't account for, stuff that doesn't fit exactly. Homicide cases aren't neat, even the neat ones."

"You think this is a neat one?"

"In one sense," Quirk said. He looked at the pictures on the plastic cube while he talked. He was not so much weary as calm. He'd seen too much, and it had left him with that cop calm that some of them get — not without feeling, really, but without excitement.

"We have an explanation for it that works. It's not laying around loose — except that we don't have the perpetrator."

"Perpetrator," I said admiringly.

"I been watching a lot of those reality cop shows," Quirk said.

"Her husband wants the guy caught," I said.

"Sure he does," Quirk said. "Me too."

"You can't find a motive," I said.

Quirk shook his head.

"This broad is Mary Poppins, for crissake. Mother of the year, wife of the decade, loyal friend, good citizen, great human being, dedicated teacher, accomplished cook, and probably great in the sack."

"Never is heard a discouraging word," I said.

"None," Quirk said. "Nobody had a reason to kill her."

"Almost nobody," I said.

"The crazed-killer thing still works," Quirk said. "It happens."

"Husband checks out?"

Quirk looked at me as if I'd asked him his sign.

"How long you think I been doing this? Who do we think of first when a wife is killed?"

"Cherchez la hubby," I said.

"Thank you," Quirk said.

"No problems between them?"

"None that he'd mention."

"He doesn't have a girlfriend?"

"Says he doesn't."

"She doesn't have a boyfriend?"

"Says she didn't."

"You able to confirm that, as they say in the papers, independently?"

"Cops aren't independent," Quirk said. "Hot dogs like yourself are independent."

"But you looked into it."

"Far as we could."

"How far is that?"

Quirk shrugged.

"These are powerful people," Quirk said. "They have powerful friends. Everybody I ask says she was a candidate for sainthood. And he is a candidate for sainthood, and the kids are a couple of saintlettes. You push people like this only so far."

"Before what?"

"Before the commissioner calls you."

"And tells you to desist?"

"And tells me that unless I have hard evidence, I should not assume these people are lying."

"And you don't have hard evidence."

"No."

"You think there's something there?"

Quirk shrugged.

"That's why you sent Tripp to me," I said.

"This wasn't a Jamaican whore got smoked in some vacant lot, twenty miles from the Harvard Club," Quirk said. "This is an upper-crust WASP broad got bludgeoned to death at one corner of Louisburg fucking Square for crissake. We got a U.S. Senator calling to follow up on our progress. I got a call from the Boston Archdiocese. Everybody says solve it, or leave it alone."

"Which isn't the way to solve it," I said.

Again Quirk was silent.

"The way to solve it is to muddle around in it and disrupt everybody's lives and doubt everything everybody says and make a general pain in the ass of yourself."

Quirk nodded.

"You can see why I thought of you," he said.

"So if Tripp doesn't want this solved, why did he hire me?"

"I think he wants it solved, but with his assumptions and on his terms," Quirk said. "He thinks he can control you."

"Somebody ought to," I said. "Any money to inherit?"

17

"A small life insurance policy, probably covered the funeral."

"No mental illness?"

"No."

"Kids?"

"Son, Loudon, Junior, twenty-two, senior at Williams College. Daughter, Meredith, eighteen, freshman at Williams."

"They seem clean?"

"American dream," Quirk said. "Dean's list for both of them. Son's on the wrestling team, and the debating team. Daughter's president of the drama club and a member of the student council, or whatever the fuck they call it at Williams."

"Any history on the kids that doesn't jibe?"

"Son had a few routine teenage scrapes. Nothing that matters. I'll give you the file," Quirk said.

"You still got a guy on it?" I said.

"Yeah, Lee Farrell," Quirk said.

"He's new," I said.

"Yeah, and he's gay."

"Young and gay," I said.

"I got no problem with it, long as he doesn't kiss me. But command staff don't like it much."

"So he gets the low-maintenance stuff."

"Yeah."

"He any good?"

18

Quirk leaned back in his swivel chair and clasped his hands behind his back. The muscles in his upper arm swelled against the fabric of his jacket.

"He might be," Quirk said. "Hasn't had a hell of a chance to prove it."

"Doesn't get the choice assignments?"

Quirk smiled without meaning anything by it.

"They had to hire him, and they had to promote him. But they don't have to use him."

"I'll want to talk with Farrell."

"Sure," Quirk said. "You and he will hit it right off."

3

Lee Farrell stopped into my office in the late afternoon while I was opening mail, and throwing it away.

"Lieutenant said you would be free-lancing the Olivia Nelson case," he said.

He was a medium-sized young guy, with a moustache, a nice tan, and the tight build of a gymnast. He was nearly bald. What hair he had was close-cropped and the moustache was neatly trimmed. He was wearing white Reeboks, and chinos, and a blue chambray shirt under a tan corduroy jacket. As he turned to sit down, the butt of his gun made an angular snag in his jacket. He shrugged his shoulders automatically to get rid of it.

"Yes," I said.

"Lieutenant said I should cooperate."

"How do you feel about that?" I said.

"Figured I could probably get by without you," Farrell said.

"It's alarming how many people think that," I said.

"No good for business," he said.

"I've read the file," I said.

"Lieutenant doesn't usually hand those out," Farrell said.

"Good to know," I said. "You got anything not in the file?"

"If I had it, it would be in there," Farrell said.

"It wouldn't have to be," I said. "It could be unsubstantiated opinion, guesswork, intuition, stuff like that."

"I deal with facts," Farrell said.

It made me smile.

"You think that's funny?" he said.

"Yeah, kind of. Are you familiar with *Dragnet*?"

"No. I don't like people laughing at me."

"Nobody does," I said. "Think of it as a warm smile of appreciation."

"Hey, asshole," Farrell said. "You think you can fuck with me?"

He stood up, his hands loosely in front of him, one above the other. He probably had some color belt, in some kind of Asian handfighting.

"Does this mean you're not feeling cooperative?" I said.

"It means I don't take smart shit from anybody. You think maybe I'm not tough enough? You can step up now and try me."

"Good plan," I said. "We beat the hell out of each other, and when the murderer dashes in to break it up, we collar him."

"Aw, hell," Farrell said. He stood for another moment, shifting a little on his feet, then he shrugged and sat down.

"I don't like being stuck on a no-brainer," he said. "They think it's a dead-file case, but they can't ignore it, so they put the junior man on it."

I nodded.

"The case stinks," he said.

I nodded again. Penetratingly.

"Everything's too perfect. No one had a bad word. Everyone liked her. No one could think of a single reason to kill her. No enemies. No lovers. Nothing. We talked with everybody in the family. Everybody at work. Everybody in her address book. Every return address on her mail. We made a list of every person we'd talked with and asked her husband and children if there was anyone they could think of not on it. We did the same at work. We got a few more names and talked with them. We do not have a single suspect out of any of them. We talked with her gyno, her physical trainer . . ." He spread his hands.

"Do you think there's something wrong," I said, "because you're stuck on a no-brainer and don't want to accept it, or is there something wrong?"

"I'm stuck on five no-brainers," Farrell

said. "I've got a full case load of cases that go nowhere."

"My question stands," I said.

Farrell rubbed his hands slowly together, and opened them and studied the palms for a moment.

"I don't know," he said. "I've thought of that too and I don't know."

4

Louisburg Square is in the heart of Beacon Hill, connecting Mt. Vernon and Pinckney Streets. In the center of the square is a little plot of grass with a black iron fence around it and a statue of Christopher Columbus. Around the square and facing it were a series of three-story, brick-front townhouses.

The Tripp-Nelson home was one of them. It had a wide raised panel door, which was painted royal blue. In the middle of the door was a big polished brass knocker in the form of a lion holding a big polished brass ring in his mouth.

I had walked up the hill from Charles Street, the way Olivia Nelson had on the night she was killed. I stopped at the lower corner of the square where it connected to Mt. Vernon. There was nothing remarkable about it. There were no blood stains, now. The police chalkings and the yellow crime-scene tape were gone. Nobody even came and stood and had their picture taken on the spot where the sixteen-ounce framing hammer had exploded against the back of Olivia Nelson's skull. According to the coroner's report she probably never knew it. She probably felt that one explosion — and the rest was silence.

I had her case file with me. There wasn't anywhere to start on this thing, so I thought it might help to be in her house when I read the file of her murder investigation. It wasn't much of an idea, but it was the only one I had. Tripp knew I was coming. I had told him I needed to look around the house. A round-faced brunette maid with pouty lips and a British accent answered my ring. She had on an actual maid suit, black dress, little white apron, little white cap. You don't see many of those anymore.

"My name's Spenser," I said. "Mr. Tripp said you'd be expecting me."

She looked at me blankly, as if I were an inoffensive but unfamiliar insect that had settled on her salad.

"Yes, sir," she said. "You're to have the freedom of the house, sir. May I take your hat, sir?"

I was wearing a replica Brooklyn Dodgers baseball cap, royal blue with a white B and a white button on top. Susan had ordered it for me at the same time she'd gotten me the replica Braves hat, which I wore with my other outfit.

"I'll keep it," I said. "Makes me look like Gene Hermanski."

"Certainly, sir. If you need me you should ring one of these bells."

She showed me a small brass bell with a rosewood handle sitting on the front hall table.

"How charming," I said.

"Yes, sir."

She backed gracefully away from me and turned and disappeared under the staircase, presumably to the servants' area below stairs. She had pretty good legs. Although in Louisburg Square it was probably incorrect to look at the maid's legs at all.

There was a central stairway in the front hall, with mahogany railing curving down to an ornate newel post, white risers, oak treads. To the right was the living room, to the left a study, straight down the hall was a dining room. The kitchen was past the stairs, to the right of the dining room. With the file under my arm, I walked slowly through the house. The living room was in something a shade darker than ivory, with pastel peach drapes spilling onto the floor. The furniture was white satin, with a low coffee table in the same shade of marble. There were rather formal-looking photographs of Tripp, a woman whom I assumed to be his late wife, and two young people who were doubtless their children.

26

There was a fine painting of an English setter on the wall over a beige marble fireplace, and, over the sofa, on the longest wall, a large painting of a dapple gray horse that looked like it might have been done by George Stubbs and selected because the tones worked with the decor.

The house was very silent, and thickly carpeted. The only noise was the gentle rush of the central air-conditioning. I had on the usual open shirt, jeans and sneakers, plus a navy blue windbreaker. It was too warm for the windbreaker, but I needed something to hide my gun; and the Dodger cap didn't go with any of my sport coats.

The study was forest green with books and dark furniture and a green leather couch and chairs. There was a big desk with an Apple word processor on one corner. It was more out of place than I was. It looked sort of unseemly there. No one had thought of a way to disguise it as a Victorian artifact.

The books were impersonal. Mostly college texts, from thirty years ago, a picture book about Frederic Remington, an American Heritage Dictionary, a World Atlas, Ayn Rand, James Michener, Tom Clancy, Barbara Taylor Bradford, Louis L'Amour, Jean Auel, Rod McKuen, three books on how to be your own shrink, and *A History of the Tripps of New*

England in leather, with gilt lettering on the spine. I put my murder file on the desk and took the book down and sat on the green leather couch and thumbed through it. It was obviously a commissioned work, privately printed. The Tripps had arrived in the new world in 1703 in the person of Carroll S. Tripp, a ship's carpenter from Surrey, who settled in what later became Belfast, Maine. His grandson moved to Boston and founded the Tripp Mercantile Company in 1758, and they had remained here since. The organizing principle of the book appeared to be that all the Tripps were nicer than Little Bo Peep, including those from the eighteenth century who had founded the family fortune by making a bundle in the rum, molasses, and slave trade business. It told me nothing about the murder of Olivia Nelson, who had kept her birth name.

5

The house was very still. The soft sound of the air conditioner made it seem stiller, and only the sound of a clock ticking somewhere in another room broke the hush.

I put the family history away and opened the case file Quirk had given me. Sitting on the green leather couch in the silent room of her nearly empty home, I read the coroner's description of Olivia Nelson's death. I read the crime-scene report, the pages of interview summaries, the document checks, I plowed through all of it. I learned nothing useful. I didn't expect to. I was simply being methodical, because I didn't know what else to be. Quirk had turned everything he had loose on this one and come up with nothing.

I put the file down and got up and walked through her house. It was richly decorated in appropriate period. Nothing didn't match. At the top of the stairs I turned right toward the master suite. The cops had already noted that the Tripps had separate bedrooms and baths. The bedrooms were connected by a common sitting room. It had a red-striped Victorian fainting couch, and two straight chairs and a leather-topped table with fat legs in front of the window. There was a copy of *Pride and Prejudice*, by Jane Austen, on the table. It seemed brand new. It was bound in red leather and matched the table top. Against the wall opposite the window was a big mahogany armoire with ornate brass hinges. I opened it. It was empty. The room was as cozy as a dental lab. I went through the sitting room to her room. It was clearly hers: canopied queen-size four poster, antique lace bedspread, heavy gathered drapes with a gold tone, thick ivory rug, on the wall at the foot of the bed a big nineteenth-century still life of some green pears in a blue and white bowl. Her bureau drawers were full of sweaters and blouses and more exotic lingerie than I'd have expected. There was a walk-in closet full of clothes appropriate to an affluent Beacon Hill pillar of the community. She had maybe thirty pairs of shoes. Her jewelry box was full. She had a lot of makeup.

I sat on her bed. It had about seven pillows on it, carefully arranged as she had left them the last time she was here, or maybe the maid had arranged them this morning. I listened to the quiet. It was a cool day outside, in the low seventies, and the air conditioner had cycled off. I was out of earshot of the clock.

I heard only the quiet, and the more I listened the more I heard it. Nothing moved. No one whispered the butler did it.

I stood up and walked across the room and through the sitting room and into Loudon Tripp's bedroom. It had been created by the same sensibility as the rest of the house. Hers, I assumed, or her decorator's. Except that it had no canopy, the big four-poster bed was identical to hers, the fluted mahogany bedposts shaped like tall Indian clubs. On the bedside table was a thick paperback copy of Scott Turow's new novel. A television remote lay next to it. There was a still life on the wall, and an identical armoire stood in the same position that it stood in Olivia's room. I opened it. There was a big-screen television set on an upper shelf, connected through a hole in the back to electrical and cable outlets behind the piece. On the lower shelves were magazines: *Sports Illustrated*, *Forbes*, *Time*, two back copies of *The New York Times Magazine*, and a current *TV Guide*. The rest of the rooms were unrevealing. The children's rooms were gender appropriate, impersonal and perfectly coordinated. There were guest rooms on the third floor.

I went back down to the living room and picked up the picture of Olivia Tripp and sat on the satin-covered couch and looked at it.

She was blonde and wore her short hair in the sort of loose blonde way that wealthy WASP women affect. Her skin looked healthy, as if she exercised out of doors. Her eyes were wide apart. Her nose was straight, and quite narrow with nostrils that flared sort of dramatically. Her mouth was a little thin, though she'd made it look more generous than it was with the judicious use of lip pencil. There was a strand of pearls just above the point where her neck disappeared into airbrushed gossamer. She looked to be in her early forties.

She was forty-three when she died. Not planning to, no time to get ready for it, walking along in her good clothes, maybe a small aftertaste of Oreo cookie in her mouth, maybe thinking about her children, or her husband, or sex, or sleep, or good works, maybe trying to remember the lyrics to a song by Harry Belafonte. And somebody appearing in the shadows, faceless and silent in the quiet summer night, with a long-handled hammer. Like an old stone-age savage, armed.

But that was to come. The face in the expensive portrait showed no hint of that. It looked out at me tranquil and personless, and devoid of meaning.

"What the hell are you looking at?" a voice said, and I looked up, and there were the children.

6

She was cute. Short, trim body, blonde pony tail, big violet eyes, lips that looked slightly swollen. She wore too much makeup, and there was something about her bearing that murmured *don't look at me,* at the same time that the makeup and the clothes were shouting *see me!* She stood slightly behind her brother, her eyes fixed on the coffee to the right of me.

"My name's Spenser," I said. "I'm a detective."

She was wearing a white tank top and pink short-shorts and thick white socks and white training shoes with pink laces. She had an immaculate tan.

Her brother looked just like her, except he wasn't cute. And he wasn't self-effacing. He wasn't short either, probably 5'11", but he had the thick wrestler's neck and upper body, and it made him look shorter than he was. He had the pouty lips too. His nose was too small for his face. His eyes were set in deep sockets. His blond hair was cut short, except in front where it was longish and combed back. He looked petulant and angry. It might have been me, but I suspected that it was his permanent expression. He wore a rust tank top and white shorts and gray socks and white high-cut basketball shoes. Rust-rimmed sunglasses with dark green lenses hung on a rust-and-white braided cord from around his neck. His tan was immaculate too.

The two of them stood very close together as they looked at me. Ken and Barbie. Except Barbie wouldn't look at me.

"Put the picture down," he said. "Who the hell let you in here?"

"Your father," I said. "He hired me to find who killed your mother."

"Swell," the brother said, "we don't have enough half-arsed cretin cops slopping around. Dad has to hire an extra one."

"You're Meredith," I said to the sister.

She nodded.

"And you're Loudon, Junior," I said.

He didn't say anything.

"Sorry about your mother," I said.

"Great," he said. "Now why don't you just get lost?"

"Why so hostile?" I said.

"Hostile? Me? If I get hostile, brother, you'll goddamn well know about it."

"Chi-ip," Meredith said. Her voice was very soft.

"Your father probably needs to do this," I said.

"Yeah," Chip said. "Well, I don't like you looking at my mother's picture."

His stare was full of arrogance. It came with wealth and position. And it came with being a wrestler. He thought he could toss me on my kiester.

If I kept talking to them he was going to try it, and find he had misjudged. It would probably be a good thing for him to learn. But now was probably not the best time for him to learn it.

I put the picture down carefully on the table and stood.

"I'm afraid I'll have to keep looking into this. I'll try not to be more annoying than I have to be."

Meredith said, in a voice I could barely hear, "You might make everything worse."

"You better keep your hands off my mom's stuff," Chip said.

I smiled graciously, and went past them and out the front door. It wasn't much of a move, but it was better than wrestling with Chip.

7

I met Lee Farrell in a place called Packie's in the South End. He was alone at the bar when I came in. He had a half-drunk draft beer in front of him and an empty shot glass.

I slid onto the bar stool and looked at the shot glass.

"Old Thompson?" I said.

"Four Roses," he said. "You got a problem with that?"

"Nostalgia," I said. "When I was a kid it was a Croft Ale and a shot of Old Thompson."

"Well, now it's not," Farrell said.

"Jesus," I said, "how old were you when you dropped out of charm school?"

The bartender came down and poured another shot into Farrell's glass. He looked at me.

"Draft," I said. He drew one and put it on a napkin in front of me.

Farrell took in about half his whiskey, washed it down with some draft beer. Then he shifted on the bar stool and leaned back a little and stared at me.

"You got a reputation," he said. "Tough guy."

"Richly deserved," I said.

"Smart too," Farrell said.

"But modest," I said.

It was a little past five-thirty in the evening and the bar was lined with people. Made you wonder about the work people did if they had to get drunk when they finished.

"Quirk says you get full cooperation," Farrell said. His speech wasn't slurred, but there was a thickness to his voice. "Says you're pretty good, says you might come up with something, if there's anything to come up with."

I nodded and sipped a little beer.

"Sort of implies that I won't," Farrell said. "Doesn't it? Sort of implies that maybe I'm not so good."

"You got other things to do. I don't."

Farrell emptied his shot glass, and drank the remainder of his beer. He nodded toward the bartender, who refilled him. There was a flush on Farrell's cheeks, and his eyes seemed bright.

"How many people in this room you figure are gay?" he said.

I glanced around the room. It was full of men. I swallowed a little more beer. I looked at Farrell and shrugged.

"Everybody but me," I said.

"Pretty sure you can tell by just looking?"

"It's a gay bar," I said. "I know you're gay. Quirk told me."

"I'm not so sure I like that," Farrell said.

"Why, is it a secret?"

"No, but why is he talking about it?"

"As an explanation of why you might be stuck on a dead end case."

"I never thought Quirk cared."

"I don't think he does."

"Lotta people do," Farrell said.

"True," I said.

We sat for a while.

"You figure fags got no iron?" Farrell said.

"I assume some do and some don't," I said. "I don't know enough about it to be sure."

We sat some more.

"I'm as good as any cop," Farrell said.

I nodded encouragingly.

"Good as you too," Farrell said.

"Sure," I said.

Farrell drank more whiskey. His speech was still fully formed, but his voice was very thick.

"You believe that?" he said.

"I don't care," I said. "I don't care if you are as good as I am or not. I don't care if you're tough or not, or smart or not. I don't care if you are gay or straight or both or neither. I care about finding out who killed that broad with a framing hammer, and so far you're not helping me worth shit."

Farrell sat for a while staring at me, with the dead-eyed cop that all of them perfect, then he nodded as if to himself. He picked up the whiskey and sipped a little and put the glass down.

"You know," he said, "sometimes if I'm alone, and there's no one around . . ."

He glanced up and down the bar and lowered his voice.

". . . I order a sloe gin fizz," he said.

"A dead giveaway," I said. "Now that we've established that you're queer and you're here, can we talk about the Nelson case?" I said.

"You got the case file," Farrell said.

"Yeah, and I've seen the house, and I've talked to the children."

"Always a good time," Farrell said. The bartender came down and looked at Farrell's drink. Farrell shook his head.

"They're under stress," I said.

"Sure," Farrell said.

"Tripp and his wife had separate rooms," I said.

"Yeah."

"Which doesn't mean they didn't get along," I said.

"True."

"What do you think?"

"Hers doesn't look like she spent much time there," Farrell said.

"What's he do?" I said.

"For work?"

"Yeah."

Farrell shrugged. "Runs the family money, I guess. Got an office and a secretary in the DePaul Building downtown. Goes there every day. Reads the paper, makes some calls, goes over to Locke's for lunch."

"Nice orderly life," I said.

"Maybe it was just a random crazy," Farrell said.

"Maybe. But if we assume that, we got no place to go," I said.

"So you assume it's not random. Where does that leave you?"

"Looking for a motive," I said.

"We been over that," Farrell said. "Me, Belson, Quirk, everybody. You going to go over it again?"

"Probably," I said. "And then, probably, I'll try it from the other end."

"Her past?"

"If it's not a random killing, there's something in her life that caused it. You people have been all over the recent events. I'll go over them again because I'm a methodical guy. But I don't expect to find something you missed. On the other hand, you haven't turned out all the pockets of her history. You don't have the budget."

"But you do?"

"Tripp does," I said.

"Until he decides you're just churning his account," Farrell said.

"Until then," I said.

We sat for a while in the crowded bar. It was full of men. Most of them were in suits and ties. Some were holding hands. A tallish guy with a thin face had his arm around a gray-haired man in a blue blazer. No one paid me any mind.

"You married?" Farrell said.

"Not quite," I said.

Farrell looked past me at the bar scene.

"How about you?" I said.

"I'm with somebody," Farrell said.

We were quiet again. People circulated among the tables. I watched them, and nursed my beer.

"You notice nobody comes over," Farrell said.

"They know you're a cop," I said. "They figure I'm from the outside. They don't want to out you in case you're *en closet.*"

"On the money," Farrell said.

I waited. Farrell stared at the crowd.

"I come on too strong about things," Farrell said.

"True," I said.

"You understand why."

"Yeah."

Farrell shifted his eyes toward me and nodded several times.

"I'm sorry," he said finally.

"Okay," I said. "But I don't think I want to go steady."

8

Tripp's secretary was named Ann Summers. It said so on a nice brass plate on her nice dark walnut desk. She was probably forty-five, and elegant, with dark auburn hair worn short. Her large round eyes were hazel. And her big round glasses magnified the eyes very effectively. The glasses had green rims. She wore a short gray skirt and a long gray jacket. She was sitting, with her legs crossed, tilted back in a swivel chair, turned toward the door. Her legs were very good.

On her desk was an in-basket, empty, and an out-basket with a letter in it. There was also a phone, a lamp with a green glass shade, two manila file folders, and to one side a hardback copy of a novel by P.D. James.

"Good morning," she said. Her voice was full of polished overtones. She sounded like she really thought it was a good morning, and hoped that I did too.

I told her who I was. She seemed thrilled to meet me.

"Mr. Tripp is at his club," she said. "I'm sure he didn't realize you were coming."

She was wearing taupe hose that fitted her legs perfectly.

"Actually I'd just as soon talk with you," I said.

She lowered her eyes for a moment, and smiled.

"Really?" she said.

I was probably not the first guy to say that to her, nor, in fact, the first guy to mean it. I hooked a red leather side chair over to her desk and sat down. She smiled again. Ready to help.

"You know I'm looking into Mrs. Tripp's murder?"

"Yes," she said. "How terrible for them all."

"Yes," I said. "How's business?"

She shifted slightly in her chair.

"I beg your pardon?" she said.

"How's business here?" I said.

"I . . . I don't see why you ask."

"Don't know what else to ask," I said.

"I've talked with the police," she said. Her big eyes looked puzzled but hopeful. She'd like to help, but how?

"I know," I said. "No point in saying all that again. So we'll talk about other stuff. Like business. How is it, are you busy?"

She frowned. Conflicting emotional states were a breeze for her. A pretty frown, an un-

44

derstated hip wiggle, a slight shift in her eyes. It was beautiful to see.

"It . . . it's not that kind of business."

"What kind?"

"The kind where you can say *how's business?*" she said and smiled so warmly that I almost asked her to dance.

"Are you busy?" I said.

"Well, no, not in a regular business sense."

"What are your hours?"

"Nine to four," she said.

"And Mr. Tripp?"

"Oh, he's usually here when I arrive, and he frequently leaves after I do. I've offered to come earlier and stay longer, but Mr. Tripp says that is not necessary."

"Is he busier than you are?"

"I . . . well, frankly, I don't see why he would be."

"And how busy are you?"

She shrugged and spread her hands. Her nails were beautifully manicured and painted a pale pink.

"There are some phone calls, there are some letters. Sometimes I make restaurant reservations, sometimes travel arrangements . . ." She paused. "I read a great deal."

"Good for the mind," I said. "They eat out a lot?"

"Mr. Tripp has lunch with people nearly every day."

"Dinner?"

"I rarely make dinner reservations," she said.

"They travel much?"

She uncrossed her legs, and crossed them the other way. When she had them recrossed, she smoothed her skirt along the tops of her thighs.

"Mostly I make arrangements for the children, during school vacations."

"They do a lot of that?"

"Oh, yes, they're very well traveled. Vail or Aspen usually, in the winter. Europe sometimes, during summer vacations. And they were always flying off to visit friends from college."

"Family travel much together?" I said.

"Mr. Tripp and the children would sometimes go places, especially when the children were small."

"Ms. Nelson?" I said.

"I don't think Ms. Nelson liked to travel," she said.

I sat for a while and chewed on that. Anne Summers sat quietly, pointing her stunning knees at me: alert, compliant, calm, and stunning.

"And Mr. Tripp comes here early, and

leaves late, even though there's not much work to do?"

She nodded.

"What do you think of that?" I said.

She paused for a moment, and bit her lower lip very gently, for a moment. Then she shook her head.

"I am Mr. Tripp's employee. I like to think also that I am his friend. In either capacity I am entirely loyal to him," she said. "I would not speculate about his personal life."

"Not even to me," I said, "after what we've meant to each other?"

Ann Summers shook her head slowly.

Her smile was warm. Her teeth were very white and even. Her eyes were lively, maybe even inviting. There was something about her that whispered inaudibly of silk sheets and lace negligees, some unarticulated hint of passion, motionless beneath the flawless tranquility of her appearance. I sat for a moment and inhaled it, admired it, contemplated the clear, unexpressed certainty that exotic carnal excess was mine for the asking.

We both knew the moment and understood it.

"Monogamy is not an unmixed blessing," I said.

She nodded slightly, and smiled serenely.

"Please feel free," she said, "if you need

anything else . . ." She made a little flutter with her hands.

I stood.

"Sure," I said. "Thanks for your help."

I was pleased that my voice didn't rasp.

At the door I looked back at her, still motionless, legs crossed, smiling. The sunlight from the east window behind her caught the red highlights in her hair. Her hands rested motionless on her thighs. The promise of possibility shimmered in the room between us for another long moment. Then I took in a big breath of air and went out and closed the door.

9

I had lunch with Loudon Tripp at the Harvard Club. In Boston there are two, one downtown in a tall building on Federal Street, and the other, more traditional one in the Back Bay on Commonwealth Ave. Despite the fact that Tripp's office was downtown about a block from the Federal Street site, he chose tradition. So did I. Instead of my World Gym tank top, I wore a brown Harris tweed jacket with a faint maroon line in the weave, a blue Oxford button-down, a maroon knit tie, charcoal slacks, and chocolate suede loafers with charcoal trim. There was a herringbone pattern in my dark gray socks. I had a maroon silk handkerchief in my breast pocket, a fresh haircut, and a clean shave. Except maybe that my nose had been broken about six times, you couldn't tell I wasn't wealthy.

Tripp was wearing a banker's gray Brooks Brothers suit with narrow lapels, and three buttons, and trousers ending at least two inches short of his feet. He had on a narrow tie with black and silver stripes, and scuffed brown shoes with wing tips. You knew he was wealthy.

Tripp shook hands democratically.

"Good of you to come," he said, although I had requested the lunch.

The Harvard Club looked the way it was supposed to. High ceilings and carpeted floors and on the walls pictures of gray-haired WASPs in dark suits. We went to the dining room and sat. Tripp ordered a Manhattan. I had a club soda.

"Don't you drink?" Tripp said. He sounded a little suspicious.

"I'm experimenting," I said, "with intake modification."

"Ah," he said.

We looked at menus. The cuisine ran to baked scrod and minute steak. The waiter brought our drinks. Tripp drank half his Manhattan. I savored a sip of club soda. We ordered.

"Now," Tripp said, "how can I help you?"

"If it is not too painful," I said, "tell me about your family."

"It is not too painful," Tripp said. "What do you wish to know?"

"Whatever you wish to tell me. Talk about them a little, your wife, your kids, what they liked to do, how they got along, anything interesting about them. I'm just looking for a place to start."

Tripp smiled courteously.

"Of course," he said.

He gestured at the waiter to bring him a second Manhattan. I declined a second club soda. I still had plenty left of the first one. Club sodas seemed to last longer than vodka martinis on the rocks with a twist.

"We were," Tripp said, "just about an ideal family. We were committed to one another, loved one another, cared about one another completely."

I nodded. The waiter brought the second Manhattan. Tripp drained the remainder of the first one and handed the glass to the waiter. The waiter completed the exchange and moved away. Tripp stared at the new Manhattan without drinking any.

"The thing was," he said, "not only were Olivia and I husband and wife, we were pals. We enjoyed each other. We enjoyed our children."

He paused, still staring at the untouched drink in front of him. He shuddered briefly. "To have so good a thing shattered so terribly . . ."

I waited. He picked up the Manhattan and took a small sip and replaced it. I ignored my club soda.

"I know it sounds, probably, too good to be true, nostalgia or something, but, by golly, it was good. There'll never be anyone like her."

He broke off and we sat quietly. In the silence the waiter brought our lunch. I had opted for a chicken sandwich. Tripp had scrod. The food was every bit as good as it was at the Harvard Faculty Club where I had eaten a couple of years ago.

There weren't many women in the dining room. At a table next to the wall two men in suits were ordering more drinks. One of them was a U.S. Senator, still pink from the steam room, whose drink, when it arrived, appeared to be a tall dark scotch and soda. At the table next to me were three guys dressed by the same costumer. All wore dark blue suits with a thin chalk stripe, white shirts with discreetly rolled button-down collars, red ties. The ties varied — one red with tiny white dots, one a darker red with blue stripes, one blue paisley on a red background. He who would be a man must be a non-conformist. One of them was holding forth. He was large without being muscular, and his neck spilled out a little over his collar.

"So there's Buffy," he was saying, "bare ass in the middle of the fucking tennis court, and . . ."

"I suppose it seems idealized to you," Tripp said. "I imagine people tend to talk that way after a great loss."

"I just listen," I said.

"And make no judgments?"

"Open-shuttered and passive," I said. "Not thinking, merely recording."

"Always?"

"At least until all the precincts are heard from," I said.

"I would find that difficult, I guess," Tripp said.

I chewed on my chicken sandwich. The chicken had traveled some distance from the coop. The slices in my sandwich were perfectly round and wafer thin. But the bread was white, and the pale lettuce was limp.

I finished chewing and said, "What I do requires a certain amount of distance, sort of a willful suspension, I suppose."

"A what?"

I shook my head. "Literary allusion," I said. "I was just showing off."

"Olivia was a great one for that. She was always quoting somebody."

"She taught literature, did she not?"

"Yes, and theater, at Shawmut College. Her students loved her."

I nodded. I was trying to pick up the conversation at the next table. They were discussing what Buffy had tattooed on her buttocks.

"She was a marvelous teacher," Tripp said. He was eating his scrod at a pace that would take us into the dinner hour. If he and Susan had an eating race you couldn't get a winner.

The Senator had finished one dark scotch and soda, and had another, partly drunk, in his left hand. He was table-hopping. At the table next to us he paused long enough to hear the end of Buffy's adventure, and laughed and said something in an undertone to the story teller. The whole table laughed excessively. It was clannish laughter, the laughter of insiders, us boys. It was almost certainly laughter about the aptly named Buffy. Men never laughed quite that way about anything but women in a sexual context. And it was sycophantic laughter, tinged with gratitude that a man of the Senator's prominence had shared with them not only a salacious remark but a salacious view of life.

"Old enough to bleed," the Senator said, "old enough to butcher."

The table was again frantic with grateful hilarity as the Senator turned toward us. The pinkness in his face had given way to a darker red. A tribute perhaps to the dark scotch and soda. He was nearly bald but had combed his hair in the bald man's swoop up from behind one ear, arranged over the baldness, and lacquered in place with hair spray. A smallish man, he looked in good shape. His three-piece blue suit fit him well, and his vest didn't gap — no mean achievement in a politician. When he turned toward us, his expression was grave. He put a hand on Tripp's shoulder.

"Loudon," he said. "How you holding up?"

Tripp looked up at the Senator and nodded.

"As well as one could expect, Senator, thanks."

The Senator looked at me, but Tripp didn't introduce us.

"I'm Bob Stratton," the Senator said, and put out his hand. I said my name and returned his handshake. If he really saw me at all, it was peripherally. In his public self he probably saw everything peripherally. His focus was him.

"Any progress yet in finding the son of a bitch?"

Tripp shook his head.

"Not really," he said. "Spenser here is working on it for me."

"You're a police officer?" the Senator said.

"Private," I said.

"Really?" he said. "Well, you need any doors open, you call my office."

"Sure," I said.

"You have a card?" the Senator said. "I

want to alert my people in case you need help."

I gave him a card. He looked at it for a moment, and nodded to himself, and put the card in his shirt pocket. And put his hand back on Tripp's shoulder.

"You hang tough, Loudon. Call me anytime."

Tripp smiled wanly.

"Thanks, Senator."

The Senator squeezed Tripp's shoulder and moved off toward another table, slurping a drink of dark scotch and soda as he went.

"Fine man," Tripp said. "Fine Senator, fine man."

"*E pluribus unum*," I said.

10

I never saw Susan without feeling a small but discernible thrill. The thrill was mixed with a feeling of gratitude that she was with me, and a feeling of pride that she was with me, and a feeling of arrogance that she was fortunate to be with me. But mostly it was just a quick pulse along the ganglia which, if it were audible, would sound a little like *woof*.

She was as simply dressed tonight as she ever got. Form-fitting jeans, low black boots with silver trim, a lavender silk blouse partly buttoned over some sort of tight black undershirt. She had on jade earrings nowhere near as big as duck pins, and her thick black hair was short and impeccably in place.

"You look like the cat's ass tonight," I said.

"Everything you say is so lyrical," Susan said. She had a glass of Iron Horse champagne, and had already drunk nearly a quarter of it, in barely twenty minutes. "What's for eats?"

"Buffalo tenderloin," I said, "marinated in red wine and garlic, fiddle head ferns, corn pudding, and red potatoes cooked with bay leaf."

"Again?" Susan said.

Pearl the wonder dog was in the kitchen with me, alert to every aspect of the buffalo tenderloin. I sliced off an edge and gave it to her.

Susan came and sat on a stool on the living room side of the counter. She drank another milligram of her champagne. She took the bottle out of the glass ice bucket on the counter and leaned forward and filled my glass.

"Paul telephoned today," she said. "He said he'd tried to get you but you were out."

"I know," I said. "There's a message on my machine."

"He says the wedding is off."

I nodded.

"Did you know?"

"He'd been talking as if it wouldn't happen," I said.

"He had a difficult childhood," Susan said.

"Yeah."

"You disappointed?"

I nodded.

"You know how great I look in a tux," I said.

"Besides that."

"People shouldn't get married unless they are both sure they want to," I said.

"Of course not," Susan said.

"Would have been fun, though," I said.

"Yes."

There was a fire in the living room fireplace. The smell of it always enriched the apartment, though less than Susan did. Outside the living room windows opposite the counter, the darkness had settled firmly into place.

I took a small glass tray out of the refrigerator and put it on the counter.

"Woo woo," Susan said. "Red caviar."

"Salmon roe," I said. "With toast and some crème fraîche."

"Crème fraîche," Susan said, and smiled, and shook her head. I came around from the kitchen and sat on the other stool, beside her. We each ate some caviar.

"You're working on that murder on Beacon Hill," she said.

"Yeah. Quirk sent the husband to me."

"Because?"

"The husband wasn't satisfied with the police work on the case. Quirk had gone as far as he could."

"Was Quirk satisfied with the police work on the case?" Susan said.

"Quirk doesn't say a hell of a lot."

"He isn't satisfied, is he?" Susan said.

"The official explanation," I said, "is that Olivia Nelson was the victim of a random act of violence, doubtless by a deranged person. There is no evidence to suggest anything else."

"And Quirk?"

"He doesn't like it," I said.

"And you?"

"I don't like it," I said.

"Why?"

One of the many things about Susan that I admired was that she never made conversation. When she asked a question she was interested in the answer. Her curiosity was always genuine, and always engendering. When you got through talking with her you usually knew more about the subject than when you started. Even if it was your own subject.

"She was beaten to death with a framing hammer. She had one bruise on her shoulder where she probably flinched up," I demonstrated with my own shoulder. "And all the rest of the damage was to her head. That seems awfully careful for a deranged killer."

"Derangement can be methodical," Susan said.

I nodded and drank some champagne. I put some salmon caviar on a triangle of toast and spooned a little crème fraîche on top. I held it toward Susan, who leaned forward and bit off the point. I ate the rest.

"And," I said, "despite what people think, there aren't that many homicidal maniacs roaming the streets. It's never the best guess."

"True," Susan said. "But it is possible."

"But it's not a useful hypothesis, because it offers no useful way to proceed. The cops have already screened anybody with a record on this kind of thing. Beyond that all you can do is wait, and hope to catch him next time. Or the time after that."

The fire softened the room as we talked. Fire was the heart of the house, Frank Lloyd Wright had said. And if he didn't know, who would.

"But," Susan said after she thought about it, "if you assume that it's not a madman . . ."

"Madperson," I said.

Susan put a hand to her forehead.

"What could I have been thinking?" she said. "If you assume it is not a madperson, then you can begin to do what you know how to do. Look for motive, that sort of thing."

"Yes," I said.

Susan still had half a glass of champagne, but she added a splash from the bottle to reinvigorate it. While she did that I got up and added two logs to the fire.

"Still there's something else," Susan said.

"Just because you're a shrink," I said, "you think you know everything."

"I think I know you," she said, "and it has nothing to do with my profession."

"Good point," I said.

I drank some champagne and ate salmon

roe, and thought how to phrase it. Susan was quiet.

"It's that there's an, I don't know, an official version of everything. But the objective data doesn't quite match it. I don't mean it contradicts it, but . . ." I spread my hands.

"For instance," Susan said.

"Well, the home. It's lovely and without character. It's like a display, except for his bedroom; it's as personless as a chain hotel."

"His bedroom?"

"Yeah. That's another thing. They have separate bedrooms separated by a sitting room. His shows signs of use — television set, some books on the bedside table, *TV Guide*. But hers . . ." I shook my head. "The kids' rooms are like hers. Officially designated children's rooms, and appropriately decorated. But no sense that anyone ever smoked a joint in there or read skin magazines with a flashlight under the covers."

"What else?"

"He goes to the office every day early, stays late. There's nothing to do. His secretary, who is, by the way, a knockout, is catching up on her reading."

"This is subtle," Susan said.

"Yeah, it is, though it's not quite as subtle when you're experiencing it. He talks about his children without any sense that now and then they might, or might have sometime, driven him up the wall. They're perfect. She was perfect. His love was all-encompassing. His devotion is unflagging."

"And there's a legal limit on the snow here," Susan said.

I nodded. "Yeah."

"That Camelotian hindsight is not unusual in grief," Susan said.

"I know," I said. "I've seen some grief myself."

"It's a form of denial."

"I know. What I'm trying to get hold of is how long the denial has been going on."

"Yes," Susan said.

"And what's being denied," I said.

Susan nodded. The fire hissed as some sap boiled out of the sawn end of one of the logs. The salmon caviar was gone. The champagne was getting low.

"So what are you going to do?" Susan said.

"Start from the other end."

"You mean look into her past?"

"Yeah. Where she was born. Where she went to school, that stuff. Maybe something will turn up."

"Wouldn't the police have done that?" Susan said.

"On a celebrity case like this, with an uncertain victim, maybe," I said. "But this victim is a well-known pillar of the community. Her life's an open book. They haven't the money or the reason to chase her back to her childhood."

"So why will you do it?" Susan said.

"I don't know what else to do," I said. "You want to eat?"

Susan drank some of her champagne and looked at me over the rim of her glass.

"How attractive was Tripp's secretary, exactly?" Susan said.

"Quite," I said.

Susan smiled.

"How nice," she said. "Perhaps after we've eaten buffalo tenderloin and sipped a dessert wine on the couch and watched the fire settle, you'll want to think about which of us is, or is not, going to ball you in the bedroom until sunrise."

"You're far more attractive than she is, Buffalo gal," I said.

"Oh, good," she said.

We were quiet as I put the meat on the grill and put the corn pudding in the oven.

"Sunrise?" I said.

"The hyperbole of jealous passion," Susan said.

11

I sat with Lee Farrell in the near empty squad room at Homicide. Quirk's office was at the far end of the room. The glass door had *Commander* stenciled on it in black letters. Quirk wasn't there. There was only one cop in the squad room, a heavy bald guy with a red face and a big belly, who had a phone shrugged up against his ear and his feet up on the desk. A cigarette with a long ash hung from his mouth and waggled a little as he talked. Ash occasionally fluttered off the end and flaked onto his shirt front. He paid it no mind. He had his gun jammed inside his belt in front, and it was obviously digging into him while he sat. Two or three times he shifted to try and ease it, and finally he took it out and put it on his desk. It was a Glock.

"Everybody got Glocks now?" I said.

"Yeah," Farrell said. "Department's trying to stay even with the drug dealers."

"Succeeding?"

Farrell laughed. "Kids got Glocks," he said. "Fucking drug dealers have close air support."

The fat cop continued to talk. He was animated, waving his right hand about as he talked. When the cigarette burned down, he spat it out, stuck another one in his mouth and lit it with one hand.

"The background stuff on Olivia says she was born in Alton, South Carolina, in 1948," I said.

"Yeah."

"Father and mother deceased, no siblings."

"Yeah."

"BA, Duke, 1969; MA, Boston University, 1982."

Farrell nodded. While I talked he unwrapped a stick of gum and shoved it in his mouth. He didn't offer me any.

"Taught Freshman English classes parttime at Shawmut College, gave an Art Appreciation course at Boston Adult Ed in Low Country Realism."

"Whatever that is," Farrell said.

"Vermeer," I said, "Rembrandt, those guys."

"Sure," Farrell said. He chewed his gum gently.

"Worked on the last couple of Stratton campaigns, volunteered on the United Fund, and a bunch of other charities."

"Okay," Farrell said, "so you can read a report."

"And that's it?"

"You got the report," Farrell said.

"Anybody go down to Alton?"

Farrell stared at me.

"You heard about the state of the economy around here?" he said. "I gotta work extra detail to fucking buy ammunition. They're not going to send anybody to Alton, South Carolina, for crissake."

"Just asking," I said.

"I made some phone calls," Farrell said. "They've got a birth certificate on her. The Carolina Academy for Girls has her attendance records. Duke and BU both have her transcripts."

"Perfect," I said.

"You going to go down?" Farrell said.

"Probably," I said. "I'm getting nowhere up here."

"Join the group," Farrell said. "Incidentally, we got an inquiry on you from Senator Stratton's office."

"If nominated I will not run," I said. "If elected I will not serve."

Farrell ignored me.

"Came into the commissioner's office, and they bucked it on down to me."

"Because he mentioned the Nelson case?"

"Yeah. Commissioner's office never heard of you."

"Their loss," I said. "What did they want to know?"

"General background, my impressions of your competence, that stuff."

"Who did you talk to?"

"Guy named Morrissey, said he was the Senator's aide."

"What did you tell them?"

"Said you were cute as a bug's ear," Farrell said.

"You guys," I said, "are obsessed with sex."

"Why should we be different?"

12

I flew to Atlanta the next morning, took a train from the gate to the terminal, got my suitcase off the carousel, picked up a rental car, and headed southeast on Route 20 toward Alton. Most of the trip was through Georgia, Alton being just across the line in the western part of South Carolina, not too far from Augusta. I got there about two-thirty in the afternoon with the sun shining heavy and solid through the trees that sagged over the main road.

It was a busy downtown, maybe two blocks wide and six blocks long. The first building on the left was a three-story white clapboard hotel with a green sign that said *Alton Arms* in gold lettering. Across the street was a Rexall drugstore and lunch counter. Beside it was a men's clothing store. The mannequins in the window were very country-club in blue crested blazers and plaid vests. There were a couple of downscale restaurants redolent of Friolator, a store that sold yarn, and a big Faulknerian courthouse made out of stone. The cars parked nose in to the curb, the way they do in towns, and never do in cities.

I parked, nose to curb, in front of the Alton Arms, and walked around a Blue Tick hound sleeping on the hot cement walkway in the sun. His tongue lolled out a little, and his skin twitched as if he were dreaming that he was a wild dog on the East African plains, shrugging off a tsetse fly.

The lobby was air-conditioned, and opened into the dining room, up one step and separated by an oak railing. At one end of the room was a fireplace sufficient to roast a moose, to the left of the entrance was a reception desk, and behind it was a pleasant, efficient-looking woman with silvery hair and a young face.

Her looks were deceptive. She was as efficient as a Russian farm collective, although probably more pleasant. It was twenty minutes to register, and ten more to find a room key. By the time she found it I had folded my arms on the counter and put my head down on them.

She was not amused.

"Please, sir," she said. "I'm doing my best."

"Isn't that discouraging," I said.

When I finally got to my room, I unpacked. I put my razor and toothbrush in on the bathroom counter, put my clean shirt on the bureau, and put the Browning 9mm on my belt, back of my hip bone, where the drape of my jacket would hide it in the hollow of my back. Nice thing about an automatic. Being flat, it didn't compromise any fashion statement that you might be making.

I had considered risking Alton, South Carolina, without a gun. But one of Spenser's best crime-buster tips is, never go unarmed on a murder case. So I'd packed it under my shirt, and clean socks, and checked the bag through. I'd probably need it checking out.

I got walking directions to the Carolina Academy from a polite black guy wearing a green porter's uniform, and lounging around the front porch of the hotel. The Blue Tick hound was still there, motionless in the sun, but he had turned over on the other side, so I knew he was alive.

Carolina Academy was a cluster of three white frame houses set in a lot of lawn and flower beds, on the other side of Main Street, behind the commercial block that comprised the Alton downtown.

The headmistress was a tall, angular, white-haired woman with a strong nose and small mouth. She wore a long white gauzy dress with a bright blue sash. Her shoes were bright blue also.

"I'm Dr. Pauline MacCallum," she said. She was trying, I think, for crisp and efficient,

71

but her South Carolina drawl masked the effect. She gave me a crisp, efficient handshake and gestured toward the straight-back chair with arms in front of her desk.

"My name is Spenser," I said and gave her one of my cards. "I'm trying to develop a little background on a former student, Olivia Nelson, who would have been a student here during the late fifties — early sixties — I should think."

The small name plate on the desk said *Pauline MacCallum, Ed.D.* The office was oval shaped, with a big bay window that looked out on the tennis courts beyond a bed of patient lucies. On the walls were pictures of white-gowned graduating classes.

"We provide for K through 12," Dr. MacCallum said. "What year did Miss Nelson start?"

"Don't know," I said. "She was born in 1948, and she graduated from college in 1969."

"So," Dr. MacCallum said, "if she came for the full matriculation, she would have started in 1953, and graduated in 1966."

She got up and went to a bookcase to the left of her desk, and scanned the blue leatherbound yearbooks that filled the case. On the tennis courts there was a group of young women in white tennis dresses being instructed. The coach had a good tan and strong legs, and even from here I could see the muscles in her forearms. Each of the young women took a turn returning a gentle serve. Most of them swiped at the ball eagerly, but limply, as if the racket were too heavy. Rarely did the ball get back across the net.

"I hope that's not your tennis team," I said.

"Miss Pollard is a fine tennis coach," Dr. MacCallum said. "But this is a physical education class. All our girls are required to take physical education three hours a week."

She took the 1966 Carolina Academy Yearbook out from the case and opened it and thumbed through the pictures of graduating seniors.

"Yes," she said. "Here she is, Olivia Nelson. I remember her now that I see the picture. Fine girl. Very nice family."

She walked around her desk and offered me the yearbook. I took it and looked at the picture.

There she was, same narrow nose with the dramatic nostrils, same thin mouth, shaped with lipstick even then. Eighteen years old, in profile, with her hair in a long bob, wearing a high-necked white blouse. There was no hint of Vietnam or dope or all-power-to-the-people in her face. It was not the face of someone who'd listened to Jimi Hendrix, nor smoked dope, nor dated guys who chanted, "Hell no, we won't go." I nodded my head slowly, looking at it.

The chatter beneath her picture said that her hobby was horses, her favorite place was *Canterbury Farms*, and her ambition was to be the first girl to ride a Derby winner.

"What's Canterbury Farms?" I said.

"It's a racing stable, here in Alton," Dr. MacCallum said. "Mr. Nelson, Olivia's father, was very prominent in racing circles, I believe."

"What can you tell me about her?" I said.

"Why do you wish to know?"

"She was the victim of an unsolved murder," I said. "In Boston."

"But you're not with the police?"

"No, I'm employed by her husband."

She thought about that for a bit. Outside the girls continued to fail at tennis, though Miss Pollard seemed undaunted.

"I can't recall a great deal about her," Dr. MacCallum said. "She was from a prosperous and influential family here in Alton, but, in truth, most of our girls are from families like that. She was a satisfactory student, I think. Her transcript will tell us — I'll arrange for you to get a copy — but I don't remember anything special about her."

She paused for a moment and looked out

at the tennis, and smiled.

"Of course, the irony is that I remember the worst students best," she said. "They are the ones I spend the most time with."

"You were headmistress then?" I said.

"In 1966? No, I was the head of the modern languages department," she said. "I do not recall having Olivia Nelson in class."

"Is there anything you can think of about Olivia Nelson which would shed any light on her death?" I said.

Dr. MacCallum sat quietly for a moment gazing past me, outside. Outside the girls in their white dresses were eagerly hitting tennis balls into the net.

"No," she said slowly. "I know of nothing. But understand, I don't have a clear and compelling memory of her. I could put you in touch with our Alumni Secretary, when she comes back from vacation."

I accepted the offer, and got a name and phone number. We talked a little longer, but there was nothing there. I stood, we shook hands, and I left. As I walked down the curving walk I could hear the futile bonk of the tennis rackets.

"You and me, Miss Pollard."

13

Outside the Carolina Academy I paused at the curb to let a dark blue Buick sedan cruise past me, then I crossed the street and went up the low hill past the Alton Free Library toward the Alton Arms.

The white-haired desk clerk with the young face looked at me curiously as I came in through the lobby, and then looked quickly away as I glanced at her, and was suddenly very busy arranging something on a shelf below the counter. I glanced around the lobby. There was no one else in it. I went past the elevator and walked up the stairs and went in my room.

It had been tossed. Not carefully either. The bedspread hung down longer than it had before. The pillows were disordered. The drawers were partly opened. The window shades were exactly even, which they hadn't been earlier. I checked my suitcase. Nothing was missing. There wasn't much to be missing. I looked out the window. There was a dark blue Buick parked across the street.

I thought about the Buick for a while, and

about my room being searched, and about how the desk clerk had eyed me when I came in. I looked at the door. It hadn't been forced. I thought about that. Then I went back down to the lobby and said to the desk clerk, "Has anyone been in my room?"

She jumped. It wasn't much, maybe a two-inch vertical leap, but it was a jump.

"No, sir, of course not."

"What's my room number?" I said.

She turned alertly to her computer screen.

"If you'll give me your name, sir, I'll be happy to check for you."

"If you don't know my name or room number," I said, "how do you know that no one's been in there?"

"I, well, no one goes in guests' rooms, sir."

"My watch is missing," I said. "I left it on the bureau and it's gone."

"Oh, my," she said. "Well, he wouldn't . . ."

I waited. She didn't know what to say. I had time. I didn't mind the silence. From the bar down a hallway from the dining room, I could hear a man laughing. I waited.

"I'm sure he wouldn't have stolen your watch, sir."

"Who?"

"Officer Swinny."

"A cop?"

"Yes, sir. That's the only reason I let him into your room. He's a policeman. He said it was an important police matter."

"Alton Police?"

"Yes, sir. He's a detective with the Sheriff's Department."

"You know him?"

"Yes, sir. He was in high school with my brother."

"He drive a dark blue Buick sedan?" I said.

"I don't know, sir. I didn't see him until he came in the lobby. He said it was official police business. Sedale might know about his car."

"Sedale the black guy in the green uniform?"

"Yes, sir. Officer Swinny said I wasn't to tell you. He said it was official business."

"Sure," I said. Then I smiled and looked deliberately at my watch. It was 3:10. She showed no sign that it registered.

I went out onto the wide veranda. Sedale was sweeping off the steps.

I said, "Excuse me, Sedale. You know Officer Swinny of the Alton Police?"

Sedale smiled a little.

"She can't keep a secret for shit, can she," he said.

"Not for shit," I said. "You know what kind of car Swinny drives?"

"Came here he was driving a Ford Ranger

pickup. Red one with a black plastic bed liner."

"Happen to know who owns the blue Buick parked across the street?"

Sedale looked over at the Buick and then back at me and shook his head.

"Can't say I do," he said.

"You know Swinny was in my room," I said.

"Sure," Sedale said. "I let him in."

"How come?"

"She told me to."

"You stay with him?"

Sedale shook his head again.

"Just let him in. Don't hang around cops no more than I need to."

"You know when he left?"

"Sure. Left about twenty minutes ago. 'Bout ten minutes 'fore you come back."

I looked at the Buick again. It had no telltale whip antenna. But there was a small cellular phone antenna on the back window. The windows were darkly tinted.

"Anybody in the Buick?" I said.

Sedale shrugged.

"Been parked there since I came out," he said. "You in trouble?"

"Not yet," I said. I stepped off the porch and started across the street toward the Buick. There was someone in it, and as I approached, he drove away.

14

I went back in the hotel and called Farrell in Boston. Then I got directions from Sedale and walked on down toward Canterbury Farms. The racing stable was across town, but in Alton across town was not a voyage of discovery.

It had been early fall when I left Boston. But in Alton it was late summer and the thick leaves of the arching trees dappled the wide streets with sunlight. Traffic was sparse and what there was moved easily, knowing there was no hurry. The heat was gentle and closed around me quietly without the assaultive quality it always had in midsummer cities.

Beyond the Carolina Academy, I walked past a sinuous brick wall that stood higher than my head. There were no corners, no right angles. The wall curved regularly in and bellied regularly out. At the intersection of a dirt road, the wall turned cornerlessly and insinuated itself away from me. I went down the dirt road. It was soft red dirt, and my feet made a kind of chuffing sound as I walked. Here the trees didn't droop, they stood straight and very high, evergreens, pine I supposed, with no branches for the first thirty or forty feet, so that walking down the road was like walking through a columned corridor. There was no sound except for my feet, and a locust hum that was so persistent and permanent that it faded in and out of notice. Down the road I could see the training track open up and, in the center of the infield, a vast squat tree, framed by a column of pines.

The light at the end of the tunnel.

There were hoofprints in the soft earth, then the thick sound of hoofbeats. I reached the training track. Several horses were pelting around it in the soft red clay. The exercise riders were mostly girls in jeans and boots and hard hats, with their racing crops stuck in their belts in the back and sticking up along their spines. Hundred-pound girls controlling thousand-pound animals. As I got close I could hear the horses as they gulped air in through their flared nostrils, and exhaled it in big snorts. The breathing was as regular as the muffled thud of their hooves.

To the left, about a half mile up the track, was a portable starting gate. Three or four men were gathered around it looking at the horses as they ran. One of the men was mounted on a calm, sturdy brown horse. The other three were afoot. Beyond the starting gate was a parking lot with three or four vehicles in it, and beyond the lot, to the right, was a cluster of white buildings. I walked toward it.

As I got close the guy on horseback said, "Morning."

"I need to talk to somebody in charge," I said.

"That'd be Mr. Ferguson," the man on horseback said and nodded toward one of the other men standing gazing at the horses.

"Frank Ferguson," the other man said, and put out a hand.

I introduced myself.

"Come on over to the track office," Ferguson said. "Probably got some coffee left, though it might be kinda robust by now."

Ferguson was a short guy with bow legs and a significant belly, which looked sort of hard. He had all his hair and it was gray and curly and worn long for a guy his age. He had on engineer's boots, and jeans, and a red plaid shirt and a beige corduroy jacket with leather elbow patches. He headed for the office at a quick step, and as he went he dug a curved meerschaum pipe out of his right-hand coat pocket and loaded it with tobacco from a zip leather pouch. By the time we got to the office he had the pipe in his mouth going, and the tobacco stashed back in his jacket pocket.

The office was in one end of the long stable where race horses stood in separate stalls, looking out at the world, craning their necks, chewing hay, swaying, and, in at least one case, chewing on the edge of the stall. One horse, a tall chestnut colt, was being washed by a young girl with a hose. The young girl wore a maroon tee shirt that said *Canterbury Farms* on it, and her blonde hair was braided in a long pigtail that reached to her waist. She sluiced water over the horse and then soaped him and scrubbed him into a lather with a brush, and then sluiced off the suds. The horse stood quietly and gazed with his big brown eyes at the infield of the training track. Occasionally he would shift his feet a little.

The office itself was nothing much. There were pictures of horses and owners gathered in repetitive poses in the winners' circle. There seemed to be a lot of owners. Ferguson was in most of the pictures. There was a gray metal desk in the room, and a gray metal table with some file folders on it, and a coffee machine with a half-full pot of coffee, sitting on the warming plate and smelling bad, the way coffee does that has sat for half a day on warm.

Ferguson nodded at the coffee. I shook my head. He sat at the desk, I took a straight chair and turned it around and straddled it and rested my arms on the back.

"I'm a detective," I said. "And I'm looking into the background of a woman, used to work here, woman named Olivia Nelson. Be twenty-five years ago, maybe twenty-seven, twenty-eight. You here then?"

Ferguson nodded and poured himself a virulent-smelling cup of coffee. He put in two tablespoons of sugar and two more of Cremora and stirred it while he was listening to me.

"Yes, certainly. Been in this business forty years, forty-one come next spring. Right here. Helped open the damn training track in Alton. Everybody thought they had to be in Kentucky. But they didn't and I showed 'em they didn't."

He stirred his coffee some more.

"You remember Olivia Nelson?" I said.

"Jack Nelson's kid," Ferguson said. He shook his head. "Old Jumper Jack. He was a contrivance, by God, if I ever saw one."

"Jumper?" I said.

"Jack would jump anything that had no dick," Ferguson said.

"Nice to have a hobby," I said. "What can you tell me about Olivia?"

Ferguson shrugged.

"Long time ago," he said. "She was a nice enough kid, hot walker, exercise rider, just like the kids out there now, had a thing for

84

horses. You know, young girls, like to control some big strong masculine thing between their legs."

"Nicely put," I said. "Anything unusual about her?"

"Nope, richer than most . . . why I took her on. Jack had a lot of money in my horses."

"Syndication?"

"Yessir. We got over to Keeneland, up to Saratoga to the Yearling Auctions. Buy some that look right and sell shares in them."

"Know anything about Olivia after she worked here?"

Again Ferguson shrugged and took in some pipe smoke. He was a good pipe smoker. He'd lit it with one match and kept it going without a lot of motion.

"Nope," he said. "Don't keep much track of the stable kids. I know she went off to college and her momma died . . ." He shook his head slowly. "Like to killed Jack when she died. You'd a thought he didn't care, tomcatting around the way he did, but he must of loved her in his way, a hell of a lot. He went into a real tailspin when she died. Took him couple years to get over it."

Ferguson drew on the pipe and without taking it from one corner of his mouth exhaled a small stream of smoke from the other. Then he grinned.

"Still wouldn't want to leave my daughter unattended around Jack."

I had a sensation in my solar plexus that felt like *whoops* sounds.

"What do you mean?" I said.

"Jack's nearly seventy, but if he can catch it he'll jump it," Ferguson said.

I was silent. Ferguson looked at me speculatively. He knew he'd said something. But he didn't know what it was. He waited.

"He's alive," I said.

"Was last week, anyway," Ferguson said. "Had a couple drinks with him. You got more recent information?"

I shook my head. "I'd heard he was dead."

"Well, he ain't," Ferguson said.

"I was misinformed," I said.

15

The seasons hadn't changed yet in South Carolina. The weather was still summer. But the earth's orbit was implacable and despite the temperature, the evening came on earlier than it used to. It was already beginning to darken into the cocktail hour when I left Ferguson in the track office and began to stroll toward the Alton Arms. As I came past the parking lot, I saw the blue Buick pull out of the lot and head out the paved road that ran from the stable area to the highway.

Along the dirt road, under the high pines, the evening had already arrived. The locust hum had vanished, and instead there was the sound of crickets, and occasionally the sound of night birds — which probably fed on the crickets. There was no other sound, except my footsteps in the soft earth. No one else was walking on the road. I could feel the weight of the gun on my hip. It felt nice.

Since Olivia Nelson's father wasn't dead, someone had lied to the cops. But there was no way to know whether it was Loudon Tripp; or Olivia who had lied to Loudon; or Jumper

Jack himself who had deceived his daughter.

At the hotel, I went up to my room and called Farrell.

"You got anything on that license plate?" I said.

"You're going to love this," he said. "South Carolina DMV says the plate's classified. Information about ownership on a need-to-know basis only."

"You can't show a need to know?"

"Because it's following you, or you think it is? No. If it was in a hit and run and three witnesses saw it, that's need to know."

"It's part of a murder investigation," I said.

"You say so, South Carolina DMV doesn't say so. They say I can go fry my Yankee ass. Though they said it in a nice polite southern way."

"Classified plate number is usually undercover cops," I said.

"Un huh."

"Okay," I said.

I listened to the faint hollow silence on the wire for a while.

"Okay," I said again. Farrell waited.

"I got something you're going to love too," I said.

"Yeah?"

"Olivia Nelson's father is alive."

"Yeah?"

"Control yourself," I said.

"Tripp said her parents were dead," Farrell said.

"Right," I said.

"Why would he lie?"

"Maybe he didn't lie," I said. "Maybe she told him they were."

"Why would she lie?"

"Maybe she thought they were dead," I said.

"Will you fucking stop it," Farrell said. "If her father's alive and we were told he died, somebody lied."

"Yowsah," I said. Through the window of my hotel room I could see the blue Buick, motionless under the heavy trees, across the street from the hotel.

"You going to see him?"

"Yowsah."

"You going to stop talking like the fucking end man in a minstrel show?"

"Sho 'nuff, Mr. Bones," I said. "Soon's ah do sumpin 'bout this guy that's tailing me."

"Why don't you just ignore him?" Farrell said.

"Well, for one thing, it's an open tail. Unless he's the worst cop in the old Confederacy, he means me to see him."

"Which means he's trying to scare you?" Farrell said.

"Yeah. I want to know why. And who."

"You find out, let me know," Farrell said.

"Sure," I said. " 'Less of course it's classified."

16

My rental Ford was parked in the lot at the
rear right corner of the hotel. I went out
the front door and headed for it. The guy in
the Buick could see me. And he had positioned
himself so that if I drove off he could follow.
Tailing somebody is much easier if you don't
mind them knowing.

As I started up the Ford, I could see a little
puff of heat come from the tailpipe of the
Buick. I pulled out of the driveway of the
hotel parking lot, swung around the corner,
and parked directly behind the Buick with my
engine idling. Nothing happened. I couldn't
see the interior of the Buick because of the
darkly tinted glass. I sat. Across the street the
Blue Tick hound mooched around the corner
of the hotel and sat on the top step of the
veranda with his forefeet on the next step
down. Sedale came out after a while and gave
the dog something to eat. It kept its position,
its jaw working on the scrap. Sedale picked
up a broom and began to sweep the veranda.
The place looked clean, but I suspected it was
something Sedale did when things were slow,

to keep from hanging in the lobby and chatting with the desk clerk.

The Buick sat. There was a slight tremor to its back end and a faint hint of heat shimmering from its tailpipe. I thought about whether Brooks Robinson or Mike Schmidt should be third baseman on Spenser's all-time all-star team. I was leaning toward Schmidt. Of course Billy Cox could pick it with anybody, but Schmidt had the power numbers. On the other hand, so did Eddie Matthews. In front of me the Buick slid into gear and pulled away from the curb. I followed. The Buick turned left at the end of the short street, then a sharp right, slowed at a green light, and then floored it as the light turned. I ran the red light behind him, and stayed with him as he went down an alley behind a Kroger's supermarket, and kept him in sight as he exceeded the speed limit heading out the County Road.

When we hit Route 20, he headed east, toward Columbia, going around eighty-five. The rental Ford bucked a little, but it hung with him. After ten miles of this, the Buick U-turned in an *Official Vehicles Only* turnaround, and headed back west, toward Augusta. I did the same. We slowed after a few minutes at a long upgrade. There was a ten-wheeler in the right-hand lane, and a white

Cadillac in the left lane, traveling at the same speed as the tractor. They stayed in tandem, at about forty miles an hour. We were stuck behind them. We chased along at that rate for maybe five minutes. The Buick kept honking its horn, but the Cadillac never budged. There was no sign, in the Caddy, of the driver's head above the front seat. This is not usually a good omen.

At the next exit the Buick turned off, roared down the ramp, turned right toward Eureka. I followed and almost rolled past him. He had pulled in off the highway onto a gravel service road. I actually passed it before I got a flash of blue through a screen of scrubby pine trees. I stopped, backed up, and pulled in behind him. Again we sat.

There was a blue jay flying around from scrub pine to scrub pine, looking at us, and looking, also, at everything else. He would sit for a moment, his head moving, looking in all directions, then, precipitously, for no reason that I could see, he would fly to another tree, or sometimes merely flutter to another branch, and look in all directions again. *Semper paratus.*

Ahead of us the gravel road wound up toward some power lines that ran at right angles to the highway through a cut in the woods. Behind us, and above, the highway traffic swooshed by, unaware that a little ways ahead was a slow-moving road block.

Shortstop on my all-time team had to be Ozzie Smith. I'd seen Marty Marion, but he didn't hit like Ozzie. Pee Wee Reese, on the other hand, was one of the greatest clutch players I'd ever seen. That was the qualifying rule. This was an all-seen, all-time, all-star team. And Ozzie did things I'd never seen anyone do on a ball field. It had to be Ozzie.

The driver of the Buick came to a decision. The door opened and he got out and started back toward me. He had on a light beige suit and a maroon blouse with a bow at the neck, and medium high heels. He carried a black shoulder bag and he was female. Maybe forty, well built, with a firm jaw and a wide mouth. Her eyes were oval and set wide apart. Her eye makeup emphasized both the oval-ness and the spacing in ways I didn't fully understand. I rolled down my window. Her heels crunched forcefully into the gravel as she walked toward me. She seemed angry.

As she came alongside the car I said, "You ever see Ozzie Smith play?"

"Okay, pal," she said, "what's your problem?"

"Well, I'm trying to decide between Ozzie Smith and Pee Wee Reese for my all-time, all-seen team . . ."

"Never mind the bullshit," she said. "I asked you a question, I want an answer."

I smiled at her. She saw the smile, and ignored it. She did not disrobe.

"You wouldn't want to go dancing or anything, would you?" I said.

She frowned, reached in her pocket, and pulled out a leather folder. She flipped it open.

"Police officer," she said.

The shield was blue and gold and had *Alton County Sheriff* on it, around the outside.

"That probably means no dancing, huh?"

She shook her head angrily.

"Look, Buster," she said. "I am not going to fuck around with you. You answer my questions right now, or we go in."

"For what, following an officer?"

"Why you following me?"

"Because you were following me. And your license plate was classified. And I figured that if I stuck behind you, either you'd have to confront me, or I'd follow you home."

She stared at me. It was a standard cop hard look.

"You decided to confront me," I said. "Now I know you're with the Sheriff's Department. Who put you on me?"

"I'll ask the questions, Bud."

"No you won't. You don't know what to ask."

"Whether I do or not," she said, "I can tell you something. I can tell you that you are in over your head, and you'd be smart to go home and find another case before this thing gets pulled up over your ears."

"You were showing me an open tail," I said. "Somebody tossed my room, and let me know it. I figured that I was being scared off. What I want to know is, why? Who wants to discourage me? What can you tell me about Olivia Nelson? Who does your hair?" I smiled at her again.

She gave me her hard cop look again, which was surprisingly effective, considering that she looked sort of like Audrey Hepburn. Then she shook her head once, sharply. And her eyes glinted oddly.

"Rosetta's," she said, "in Batesburg."

Then she turned on her medium high heels and walked back to her car, got in, U-turned, and drove past me out onto the Eureka Road.

17

I was in my room at the Alton Arms, lying on the bed with my shoes off and three pillows propped, talking to Susan on the phone. There was a bottle of scotch and some soda and a bucket of ice on the bureau. My shirt was hung in the closet on a hanger, which had been covered with pink quilted padding. My gun was on the bedside table, barrel pointed away for good range safety. I was sipping a drink from one of the squat glasses they had sent up with the scotch. It had a crest engraved on the side with an *A* worked into it. Padded coat hangers and monogrammed glasses. First class.

"How's the baby?" I said.

"She's fine," Susan said. "I took her for a walk after work and got her a new bone and she's on the bed now, looking at me and chewing it. And getting bone juice on the spread."

"How adorable," I said. "Does she miss me?"

"Do you miss daddy, Pearl?" Susan said off the phone.

I waited.

"No," Susan said into the phone, "apparently not. Maybe after her bone is gone."

"How much crueler than the adder's sting," I said.

"I miss you," Susan said.

"That helps," I said. "But it's not the same."

"Why not?"

"You might just be driven by lust."

"Whereas Pearl's love is the stuff of Provençal poetry," Susan said.

"Exactly," I said.

She laughed. I always loved the sound of her laughter. And to have caused it was worth the west side of heaven.

"Are you having any fun down there?" Susan said.

"No. The local Sheriff's Department is attempting to frighten me to death."

"Really?"

"Yeah. I had a recent confrontation with a tough Sheriff's detective who gets her hair done at Rosetta's in Batesburg."

"Tell me," Susan said.

I did, starting with the part about the room being searched, including my conversation with Ferguson.

"So why would the Sheriff's police do that?" Susan said.

"Someone asked them to, I would guess.

I can't see why the Alton County, South Carolina, Sheriff's Department would otherwise know I existed."

"Hard to imagine," Susan said. "But probably true. So who might ask them to?"

"Somebody who doesn't want me looking into Olivia Nelson's past," I said.

"I sort of figured that out myself," Susan said. "The real question is who doesn't want you to and why not."

"Yes," I said.

"And to that question you have no answer."

"None," I said.

"Another approach might be to think who has the clout to get the Sheriff's office to do it," Susan said.

"Good thought, Della," I said.

"Della?"

"Della Street . . . Perry Mason? I guess I'm too subtle for you."

"Subtlety is not usually the difficulty," Susan said.

"Anyway," I said, "there's too much I don't know to do too much guessing. The only name that's come up, that might have the clout, is Senator Stratton."

"Why would he want to discourage you?"

"Maybe he doesn't," I said. "He knows Tripp. I met him when Tripp and I had lunch at the Harvard Club. He's inquired about me to the cops in Boston. But that may be, probably is, just a routine constituent service to a big campaign contributor, real or potential."

"But he's the only one you can think of."

"Right."

"I would think that a liberal Senator from Massachusetts wouldn't have much clout in rural South Carolina," Susan said.

"Politics make strange bedfellows," I said.

"Maybe Olivia's father who isn't dead might have had something to do with it," Susan said.

I drank some more of my scotch and soda.

"Possibly," I said.

"What are you going to do next?"

"I'm going to have a couple or three drinks," I said, "order up some sandwiches, go to bed, and sleep on it all. In the morning I'm going to the track kitchen for breakfast. Sedale, the bellhop, who is my closest personal South Carolina friend, says it's a don't-miss place where everyone eats. Authentic southern cooking, he says."

"And I'm missing it," Susan said. "What happens after breakfast?"

"I'm going to go out and see if I can talk with Jumper Jack Nelson," I said.

"That might be interesting," Susan said.

"Not as interesting as you are," I said.

"Of course not," Susan said. "But maybe

you'll find out why the police were led to believe he was dead."

"I wish you were going to be dining with me at the track kitchen tomorrow," I said. "A cup of coffee, a plate of grits, some red eye gravy, and thou."

"Assuming I could restrain my carnality," she said.

"Assuming you couldn't, we'd never be welcome at the track kitchen again."

"Take care of yourself," Susan said.

"Yes," I said. "I love you."

"I love you too," she said, "and the baby probably misses you more than she knows."

We hung up. I lay on the bed with my drink for a while looking at the little square-toothed dentil molding that went all the way around the ceiling of the room. Then I got up to freshen my drink and looked out the window. Alton was dark and silent under a dark sky. There was no moon. And no stars were visible. The wind moved the trees some, and made enough of a sound for me to hear it through the closed window. Across the street, in the yellow glare of the street lamp, there was merely an empty stretch of grass-spattered gravel. No sign of the blue Buick. No car at all. Maybe they'd given up trying to scare me. Maybe they'd just decided on a different approach. I drank my drink thoughtfully, and shrugged the bunchy muscles in my back and shoulders, and looked at the Browning lying on the night stand.

I raised my glass slightly toward the gun. "Here's looking at you, kid," I said.

Then I picked up the room service menu and began to consider my choices.

18

The track kitchen was off maybe a quarter of a mile from the Alton training track, a low, sort of white, cinder-block building with a badly defined gravel parking area in front, where there were three pickup trucks and a green Jaguar sedan. An old metal Coca-Cola sign hung over the screen door. The door hung less square than rhomboidal. The cinder block had shifted a little and everything was slightly out of plumb. Long cracks, following the right-angled joinings of the cinder block, jagged across the building front. The rich smell of lard undulated from the open windows.

I went in. The building was divided front to back into two rooms. One of the rooms contained two pool tables and a juke box. There were three or four exercise riders, in tee shirts and jeans, shooting pool and drinking Coca-Cola, and listening to Waylon Jennings. On my side of the archway, the dining area was filled with long plastic laminate tables. Across the back was the kitchen. A well-dressed man and woman were eating ham and eggs, grits, and toast at one of the tables. Three ample women in large hats and frilly dresses were at the table next to theirs. I walked back to the kitchen where two women were cooking. One of them was black and gray-haired and overweight. The other was white and gray-haired and overweight. Both had sweat beaded on their forehead. The white woman wore blue jeans more commodious than Delaware. The black woman had on a flowered dress. Both wore aprons. Without looking up from the grill, where she was scrambling some eggs, the black woman said, "Whatchu want?"

I ordered grits, toast, and coffee.

"That it?" she said.

"That's all I dare," I said. "The smell is already clogging my arteries."

Still without looking up, she tossed her head toward the formica tables. The white woman placed a large white china mug on the counter in front of me and nodded at the coffee in its warming pot.

"Have a seat," the black woman said. "We'll bring it."

I poured myself coffee, added cream and sugar, and took it with me to an empty seat. The white woman came around the counter with a startling number of plates and put them down in front of the ample women. I could see how they got ample.

I sipped some coffee. It was too hot. I swallowed the small sip with difficulty and blew on the cup for a while. Around the room there were pictures pasted up on the cinder-block wall, most of them horse racing pictures, jockeys and owners in winning circles with horses. The horses were always the least excited. They were old pictures, black-and-white blow-ups that had faded, the corners bent and torn from being repeatedly Scotch-taped to the uncooperative cinder block. The only thing recent was a big calendar for the current year, decorated with pictures of dogs playing poker. There was a picture, not recent, of Olivia Nelson, a cheap head shot in color that looked like the kind of school picture they take every year and send home in a cardboard frame and the parents buy it and put it on the mantel. I got up and went to the wall and looked more closely. Clearly it was Olivia Nelson. She looked like her yearbook picture, and she looked not too different from the picture of her at forty-two that I'd seen in her living room on Beacon Hill. My coffee had cooled a little and I drank some while I looked at her picture. The white woman came out of the kitchen and lumbered toward me with breakfast.

"Where you sitting?" she said.

I nodded at the table and she went ahead of me and set the tray down.

"Excuse me," I said. "May I ask you why you have a picture of Olivia Nelson on the wall."

The woman's gray hair was badly done up and had unraveled over her forehead like a frayed sock. She tightened her chin and her lower lip pushed out a little.

"Got no pictures of Olivia Nelson."

"Then who is this young woman?" I said, pointing to the girl in the school photo.

Her jaw got tighter and her lower lip came out a little further.

"That's Cheryl Anne Rankin," the woman said.

"She looks remarkably like Olivia Nelson, you sure it's not?"

"Guess I ought to know my own daughter," she said. Her voice was barely audible and she spoke straight down as if she were talking to her feet.

"Your daughter? Cheryl Anne Rankin, who looks just like Olivia Nelson, is your daughter?"

"She don't look like Olivia Nelson," the woman said to her feet.

I nodded and smiled engagingly. It was hard to be charming to someone who was staring at the ground.

"Do you know Olivia Nelson?"

"Used to."

"Could you tell me about her?"

"No."

"Where is your daughter now?" I said.

She shook her head doggedly, staring down.

"Got to work. Can't stand here talking the damned day away," she said.

She turned and lumbered back into the kitchen and began to break eggs into a bowl. The black woman looked at her and then glared at me. I thought about it and decided that she was reluctant to discuss it further, that her associate thought I was worse than roach turd, and that if they came at me together, I might get badly trampled.

I went back to my table and ate my grits and toast and finished my coffee and looked at the picture of Cheryl Anne Rankin, who looked just like Olivia Nelson.

I was confused.

19

Jumper Jack Nelson's house was beyond the training track, on a hill with a lawn that rolled down maybe half a mile to the roadway. The drive was crushed oyster shells, and it curved in a white arc slowly up through the putting green lawn to a porte cochere, supported on gleaming white pillars. The house too was white and looked as if it had been built before the Civil War and kept up. It was three stories, vaguely like a European country house, buoyed by foundation plantings of shrubs and flowers I didn't recognize, so that, stark white, it seemed to float atop its hill on a wave of color. The house was silent. The windows were blank, the mid-morning sun reflecting off them without meaning. At the edges of the property, on either side, tall southern pines stood, their branchless trunks like palisades containing the estate. In their branches birds fluttered. I could hear them singing. As I got closer to the house, I could see the bees hovering over the foundation plantings, moving from flower to flower. My feet seemed intrusive as I crunched up the oyster shell drive.

When I rang the bell, it chimed deep inside the house. A number of dogs barked at the sound, though not as if they meant much. I waited. The dogs continued to bark without enthusiasm, as if they were merely doing their job, and didn't really care if the doorbell rang.

A small breeze moved across the tops of the taller flowers along the front of the house and made them sway gently. The bees swayed with them, unconcerned with the breeze, focused on the nectar.

I didn't hear footsteps. The door simply opened. Slowly. A huge hallway beyond the door was dark. A slow old southern male black voice said slowly, "Yessir."

"My name is Spenser," I said and handed a card into the darkness. "I'm here to see Mr. Nelson." I smiled into the dark hallway. Friendly as a guy selling sewing machines. A black hand, nearly invisible in the dark hallway, took my card.

"Step in," the old voice said.

Inside the hallway, my eyes began to adjust. There was an odd fresh smell in the house. It was a smell I knew, but I couldn't place it. I felt something brush against my leg and looked down at an old hunting dog that was leaning against my knee. It was too dark to see him clearly, but the way he held his head, and the way his back swayed, was enough to know he was old. I reached down and let him smell the back of my hand. As my pupils continued to dilate I could see that there were three or four other dogs standing around, none of them hostile. They were all hunting dogs.

The black man said, "You wait here, sir. I'll see Mr. Nelson, can he see you."

His voice was soft, and he was very old. As tall as I was, but narrow; and stooped as if he were embarrassed to be tall and wanted to conceal it. He had on a worn black suit of some kind and a white shirt with one collar point bent upward, and a narrow ratty black bow tie, like a movie gambler, tied with the ends hanging long. The hand that held my card was surprisingly thick, with strong fingers. His hands were graceful, like he might play the harp, or deal cards.

"Sure," I said.

"Don't pay the dogs no mind, sir," he said. "They won't harm you."

"I know," I said. "I like dogs."

"Yessir," he said and moved away, his feet a whisper on the dark oak floor. He was wearing slippers.

The room was entirely dark oak, panels on the walls, panels and beams on the ceiling. There were no windows in the hall. The stairwell curved up toward the back half of the entry hall, and must have been windowed, because some light wafted dimly down from beyond the turn.

The fresh smell I'd noticed when I came in had lessened when the black man left, and as I heard his soft, whispering shuffle coming back from somewhere under the stairs it got strong again. I realized what I was sniffing. The house smelled of booze, and the black man smelled of it more so. No wonder it was familiar.

"Mr. Nelson say why you want to see him, sir?"

"It's about his daughter," I said.

"Yessir."

He shuffled away, and this time he was gone awhile. I scratched the old hound behind his ear and he leaned his head a little harder against me. The other dogs sat, respectfully, nearby, in a semicircle that probably had some dog order to it. The old one was obviously in charge. I could see well enough now to see how gray the dog's muzzle was. And around his eyes, sort of like a raccoon. His front paws turned in slightly, the way they did on a bear, and he moved stiffly.

Around the entry hall there were gilt-framed paintings of race horses, most, apparently, from the nineteenth century, when they were painted with long bodies and small heads. On the other hand, maybe in the nineteenth century they did have long bodies and small heads.

The dog nudged my knee with his head, and I reached down to pat him some more. The other dogs watched. Under the fresh booze smell was a more enduring smell of dog. I liked both smells, though there were people who liked neither.

There was no sound in the house, not even the sounds that houses make: air-conditioning, or furnace, or the stairwell creaking, or the refrigerator cycling on; nothing but a silence that seemed to have been thickening since Appomattox.

"You guys have much fun?" I said. The dogs made no reply. One of them, I didn't see which one, thumped his tail once when I spoke.

The black man scuffed quietly back into the huge entry.

"Mr. Nelson say to come this way, sir."

We went to the end of the entry hall and under the stairs and through a door into a bright gallery along the back of the house that was full of sunlight through the long bank of French windows. At the end of the gallery we turned right into a huge octagonal conservatory with a glass roof shaped like a minaret. Sitting in a wicker chaise on a dark green rug in the middle of the bluestone floor, with the sun streaming in on him, was an old man in a white suit who looked like Mark Twain gone to hell. He had long white hair and a big white moustache. He probably weighed three hundred pounds, most of it in his belly. There was some in his jowls, and plenty in the folds of his neck that spilled out over his wilted collar. But there were hints, still, as he sat there, of strength that had once existed. And in the red sagging face, the vestiges of the same profile his daughter showed in her portrait.

On the wicker table beside him was a blue pattern china bowl of melting ice, a bottle of Jack Daniel's, partly gone, and a pitcher of water. He had a thick lowball glass in his hand. A blackthorn walking stick leaned on the arm of the chaise. Across the room was a wicker chair. Next to it a wicker side table held a big color television set. On the screen stock cars, gaudily painted, buzzed endlessly around a track. There was no other furniture. The room had the feel of an empty gym.

There were three or four more dogs in here, all hunters, long eared, black and white, or blueticked, looking somewhat like Pearl the wonder dog. Except their tails were long. And the color. And they were bigger. And calmer. One of them thumped a tail on the floor when she saw me. The others watched me but did nothing. Sprawled on the floor, they moved only their eyes to look at me. Air-conditioning buzzed unseen somewhere above us. Despite the sunlight the room was cold.

The old black man gestured me to the other seat with one gnarled, still graceful hand. I sat. Jumper Jack stared at the car race. Sweat beaded on his forehead.

"Care for some whiskey and branch water, sir?" the black man said.

I thought about it. It might keep my teeth from chattering. On the other hand, it was ten-thirty in the morning. I shook my head. The black man nodded and shuffled a little ways off, near the door, and stood. Nelson continued to gaze at the stock car race.

I waited.

Nobody did anything. It was as if immobility were the natural order of things here, and movement was aberrant.

Jumper Jack drank some more whiskey.

The race announcer was frantic with excitement as the cars went round and round. The excitement seemed contrived in this room where time was suspended and movement was an oddity. The huge television set itself was inappropriate, a blatting, contemporary intrusion into this motionless antebellum room full of dogs, and old men, and me.

I sat. The black man stood. The dogs

sprawled. And Jumper Jack stared at the race and drank whiskey. I waited. I had nowhere to go.

Finally someone won the car race. Jumper Jack picked up the remote from the table beside him and pressed the mute button. The television went silent. He turned and looked at me, and when he spoke his clotted voice rumbled up out of his belly like the effortful grumble of a whale.

"Got no daughter," he said.

"None?"

"No daughter," he said and finished his whiskey and fumbled at the fixings to make another one. The old black man was there. He made the drink with no wasted movement and handed it to Nelson and returned to his motionless post near the door.

"You know a woman named Olivia Nelson?"

He shook his head, heavily, as if there were hornets around it.

"No," he said.

"Did you ever?" I said.

"No more."

"But you did once."

He looked at me for the first time, raising his head slowly from his chest and staring at me with his rheumy, unfocused gaze.

"Yes."

I waited again. Nelson drank. One of the dogs got up suddenly and walked over and put his head on Nelson's lap. Nelson automatically patted the dog's head with a thick, clumsy hand. There were liver spots on his hands and the fingernails were ragged, as if he chewed them.

"Married a African nigger," he said. "I . . ." He seemed overcome, as much by forgetfulness as by memory. He lost track of what he'd begun to say, and dropped his head and buried his nose in the lowball glass and drank.

"And?" I said.

He looked up as if he were surprised to see me there.

"And?"

"And what happened after she married?" I said.

Again his head dropped.

"Jefferson tell you," he rumbled.

I looked at the black man. He nodded.

"Jefferson," Nelson said, "you tell."

He drank again and turned the sound back on, and faced back into the car races, as if I'd vanished. His chin sank to his chest. Jefferson came over and took the whiskey glass from his hand and put it on the table. From an inside pocket he produced a big red bandanna and wiped Nelson's forehead with it. Nelson started to snore. The dog withdrew his head from Nelson's lap and went back and lay down with a sigh in the bright sun splash on the bluestone floor.

"Mr. Nelson will sleep now, sir," Jefferson said. "You and I can talk in the kitchen."

I followed Jefferson out of the cold room where Nelson lay sweating in his sleep, with his dogs, in front of the aimless car race. Despite what Ferguson said, Jumper Jack no longer seemed a danger to virgins.

20

It was a servant's kitchen, below stairs, with a yellowed linoleum floor and a big gas stove on legs, and a soapstone sink. The room was dim, and bore the lingering scent of kerosene, though I couldn't find any source for it. A mild patina of dust covered every surface. The old Blue Tick hound I'd met in the front hall followed us down to the kitchen and settled heavily onto the floor near the stove. Jefferson indicated a white metal table with folding extenders on either end, and we sat on opposite sides of it.

"Mr. Nelson has got old," Jefferson said.

"Lot of that going around," I said.

Jefferson smiled.

"Yessir," he said, "there is."

He gazed absently at the old hound lying by the stove.

"He something to see, when he younger," Jefferson said. "Ride a horse. Shoot. Handle dogs. Not afraid of any man. People step aside when he come."

Jefferson smiled softly.

"He like the ladies all right," he said.

I waited. It was a skill I was perfecting down here.

"Always took care of family," Jefferson said.

The old refrigerator in the far corner lumbered noisily into life. Nobody paid it any mind.

"Been with him all my life," Jefferson said. "He always took care of me, too."

"Now you take care of him."

"All there is," Jefferson said. "Mrs. Nelson gone. Miss Olivia gone."

"Tell me about Olivia," I said.

His voice was barely more than a whisper. His eyes were remote, his hands inert on the table looked sadly frail.

"She broke his heart," he said.

"Married a black man?"

Jefferson nodded.

"She shouldn't have done that," he said. "Broke his heart."

"Doesn't break everyone's heart," I said.

"He couldn't change, he too old, he too . . ." Jefferson thought a minute. "He too much Mr. Jack. Wasn't even one of our Nigras. Peace Corps. She marry an African Nigra."

"Did you ever meet him?" I said.

"No, sir. They never come here. Mr. Jack say he never want to see her again. Say she dead, so far as he concerned."

"And now she is," I said.

Jefferson raised his head and stared at me.

"No, sir," he said.

"Yeah. I'm sorry, Jefferson. That's why I'm looking into her past. I'll let you decide how to tell him, or if."

"When she die, sir?"

I counted in my head for a moment.

"Ten weeks ago," I said. "In Boston."

Jefferson stared at me.

"No, sir," he said.

"Sorry," I said.

"I always kept in touch with her," Jefferson said. "Mr. Jack pretends she's dead, but she writes me letter and I write her. In Nairobi — that's in Africa where she live."

I nodded. The Blue Tick hound stretched, all four legs taut for a long moment on the floor, and then lapped his muzzle once and relaxed back into sleep.

"I got a letter from her yesterday," Jefferson said.

His voice was still as ashes.

"She wrote it last week," he said. "She ain't dead, Mr. Spenser."

Nothing moved. Anywhere. It was so still I could hear the old dog breathing gently as he slept.

"You have that letter?" I said.

"Yessir."

Jefferson got up and went into a pantry and came back in a moment with a letter. It was written on that thin blue airmail stationery that folds into its own envelope and has to be slit the right way or you can't keep track of the pages.

"May I read it?" I said.

"Yessir."

The letter, addressed to *Jefferson, Dear,* was a compendium of recent activities at the medical clinic, which I gathered she and her husband operated in a Nairobi slum. AIDS was the leading killer of both men and women, she said. There were several references to Jefferson's last letter. It was dated five days previous, and signed *Love as always, Livvie.* There was no reason to doubt it.

"You'd recognize her handwriting," I said.

"Yessir. When she a little girl I help her with her homework. When she go away to college she write me every week. She been writing me every week ever since. More than twenty-five years. I know her handwriting, sir."

I nodded.

"I'm glad it wasn't her, Jefferson."

"Yessir."

"But it was somebody."

"Yessir."

I had a copy of the portrait I'd found in

the victim's living room. I took it out of my inside pocket and showed it to Jefferson.

"Sure look like Miss Livvie," Jefferson said.

"This woman said she was Olivia Nelson. She was married to a prominent Boston white man, lived on Beacon Hill, and had two college-age children."

"Can't be Miss Livvie," Jefferson said. His voice was matter of fact, the way you'd remark that the world was round.

"Do you know a woman named Cheryl Anne Rankin?" I said.

"No, sir," Jefferson said.

He was lying. He said it too quickly and with too much resolve.

"Her picture's on the wall at the track kitchen," I said. "Woman there says she's her daughter."

"Don't know nothing about that, sir."

I nodded again.

"Be all right with you, sir, you don't tell Mr. Jack I writing to Miss Livvie?"

"No need to, Jefferson," I said. "But I bet he knows anyway."

"Sure he do, sir. But he wouldn't want me to know he knows."

"You sure you don't know anything about Cheryl Anne Rankin?"

"Don't know nothing about that, sir. Nothing at all."

Jefferson stood and I stood, and we went upstairs to the front door. I put out my hand. Jefferson took it. His hand was slender and strong and dry as dust.

"Nelson is lucky to know you, Jefferson," I said.

Jefferson smiled.

"Yessir," he said.

21

The phone in my room at the Alton Arms had a long cord on it. You could stroll around the room as you talked. I was looking out my window while I told Quirk about Jefferson's story.

"You got an address for her in Nairobi?" Quirk said.

"Yeah, took it off the envelope," I said and gave it to him.

"We'll give her a call," Quirk said. "If she's actually there, we'll maybe get somebody from the American Embassy to go over and interview her."

"Farrell going to come down here?" I said.

"Somebody will," Quirk said. "Say the stuff about Cheryl Anne Rankin again."

"All I got is her picture in the track kitchen. Looks just like Olivia Nelson did in her high school graduation picture. Looks like she'd grow into that portrait in the living room in twenty-five years."

"You think they're old pictures?"

"Yeah. And the woman who says she's Cheryl Anne's mother is probably around seventy."

It was bright and hot outside the hotel window. The trees across the street seemed to hang lower than usual, and their leaves were motionless. The blue Buick pulled up as I was looking at the trees, and swung in and parked in front of the hotel. A cruiser pulled up behind it and then another one. The shield on the side said *Alton County Sheriff.* Uniformed deputies began to unload. They spread out around the hotel, trying to be inconspicuous. A couple headed around back in case I made a dash through the kitchen.

"You thinking she could be the victim?" Quirk said.

"She looks too much like the victim to ignore," I said. "But right now I got another problem."

"Yeah?"

"I think I'm going to get busted by the Alton County Sheriff's Department," I said, and described the arrivals. There was a knock on the door.

"Here they are," I said. "Tell whoever comes down to see if I'm in jail."

"I'll come down," Quirk said.

I hung up and took my gun out of my holster and laid it down on the bedside table with the muzzle facing away from the door. Then I opened the door and smiled at the cop who had her hair done in Batesburg.

22

They didn't book me. They just took my belongings, including my gun, and stuck me in a cell by myself, in the Alton County Courthouse. Nobody said anything much. But the deputies hovered close and looked as alert as they were able to, until I was locked up. Then everybody departed and I was alone in a cell about 8 by 10 feet in the cellar of the courthouse. There were no windows and only a single light in the ceiling of my cell, and one in the corridor outside. There was a toilet in the corner of the room, and a concrete bunk built out from the wall. On the bunk was a thin, bare mattress, a pillow, and a wool blanket that looked like it might once have been worn by a plow mule.

I lay on the bunk and propped the pillow under my head and looked at the ceiling for a while. There was no noise in the cell block. Either Alton County was a low-crime zone or the other prisoners were somewhere else. The arrest wasn't legal. I hadn't been charged with anything, I hadn't appeared before any magistrate, I'd not been given access to counsel. I hadn't been read my rights, probably because at the moment I didn't have any. They probably hoped that when they came, I'd resist, which would give them a charge. But I didn't. I went without a word. There was no point in asking. They wouldn't tell me. It was quite possible they didn't know. But I'd done something to motivate somebody to something, and maybe it was something stupid.

I ran over my all-time, all-seen team again: Koufax, Campanella, Musial, Robinson, Smith, Schmidt, Williams, DiMaggio, Mays. No one was out of position except Mays, and certainly Willie could play right field. And I'd have Red Barber broadcast the game. And Red Smith write about it.

The lights went out silently. The darkness was absolute. No trickle of light from anywhere until, eventually, as my eyes adjusted, I could see the hint of light from under the door to the cell block at the end of the corridor.

My basketball team was easy for the first four: Bird, Russell, Magic Johnson, and Jordan. But who'd be the other forward? Should I choose Wilt and play Russell at power forward? It seemed a cop-out. Maybe Bob Pettit. Or DeBusschere, or make Bird the power forward and play Elgin Baylor. How about Julius?

I wondered if anyone was going to give me supper, and decided that they weren't. They wanted me to be isolated and hungry and in the dark down here while my resolve atrophied. I groped to the sink next to the toilet and ran the water. There was only a cold-water faucet. I drank some from my cupped hand and began to walk back and forth in the cell, feeling for the bars and wall at first, and then, coming to know the size, keeping a hand slightly out, but walking and stopping and turning at the right time by the floor plan in my head.

I remembered the first woman I'd slept with. Her name was Lily, and I remembered her naked body in detail as explicit as if I had seen her yesterday. That was sort of interesting, so I began to remember the other women I'd slept with and found I could remember all of them exactly: how they looked, how they acted, what they said, what they liked, what they wore, and how they undressed. Some had liked me a lot, some were lost in a private fantasy and I was a vehicle for its expression, some had just liked love making, all of them had been fun.

I thought about Susan. She was the most fun.

I thought about football, and whether Joe Montana would finally replace Unitas. Jim

Brown was eternal, and certainly Jim Parker. Sarah could sing, and Mel Torme, and Dave McKenna was the piano player, and The Four Seasons, in New York, for that one meal, and Sokol Blosser Pinot Noir, and Catamount beer, and German shorthaired pointers, and Ali maybe was the best heavyweight, though Ray Robinson was, of course, the best ever, any weight, and Krug champagne, and Faulkner, and Vermeer, and Stan Kenton and Mike Royko, and fitful sleep.

23

I heard them coming and was sitting on the bunk when the lights went on and six of them came into my cell. Four of them were big Alton County Deputies with nightsticks, two of them were in suits. My friend with the hairdo and the almond-shaped eyes was not with them. All six were men.

A guy in a three-piece, blue pinstripe suit said, "On your feet, asshole."

Bust in suddenly, after hours of isolation, while I'm still asleep, scare me witless, and ask me questions. It was not a brand-new approach. I sat on the edge of my bunk with my hands relaxed in my lap and looked at him. His vest gapped at the waist, leaving two inches of badly tucked-in shirt showing over the belt line.

"On your fucking feet," he said.

"You want to wear a three-piece suit," I said, "you gotta get good tailoring. Otherwise the vest gaps."

Vest jerked his head and two deputies yanked me to my feet. I grinned at him.

"Or not," I said.

"Sit down," Vest said and shoved me with both hands. I didn't sit. I rocked back a little and kept my feet. Vest jerked his head and the same two deputies who yanked me up put a hand on each shoulder and pushed me down. I didn't go. Vest balled a fist and drove it into my stomach. He was slow. I had time to tighten my stomach and keep it from doing full damage. But it staggered me enough so that the deputies could push me down. I sat.

"Who's your trainer?" I said. "Mary Baker Eddy?"

He didn't know who Mary Baker Eddy was, but he tried not to let it show. His partner, wearing a seersucker suit and a straw snap brim with a colorful band, stood against the far wall with his arms crossed. Neither one showed a badge.

"We don't care," the partner said, "if you're a smart ass, or not. We'll take that out of you. Sooner or later, don't matter none to us. But we'll take it out of you, and you know that we can." He had a soft, almost uninflected voice, with no sign of a regional accent.

He was right. They could, and I knew it. Anybody can be softened up; it's all a matter of time and technique, and if you have the time, the technique will eventually surface. Didn't mean it had to be soon, though.

"We'd like to know," the partner said,

"what it is you're doing around here, and what you've found out about Olivia Nelson."

"You guys got any badges or anything?" I said.

In a perfectly flat and humorless voice, the partner said, "Badges, we need no stinking badges. What have you found out about Olivia Nelson?"

"She went to Carolina Academy. She liked horses," I said.

There were no other sounds here under the courthouse in the windowless room, only the sounds of our voices and the breathing of the deputies. The overhead light, unshaded and harsh, glared down at us.

"And what else?" the partner said.

He remained perfectly motionless against the wall, in a pose he'd probably practiced a thousand times. Arms folded, hat tilted over his eyes, so that the overhead light put his face in shadow.

"That's all," I said.

The room was silent.

The partner eased himself languidly off the wall and slouched over toward me. Vest gave way and moved back and replaced him on the wall. The chorus line of deputies stood motionless, while the *pas de deux* took place. The partner put a hand out toward the nearest deputy and the deputy slapped a nightstick in his hand like a scrub nurse.

"You are in so deep over your head, ass-hole," the partner said, "you're about to drown."

He was a tall man with high, square shoulders and a wide, slack mouth.

"You don't seem like you'd be an Alton County Deputy Sheriff," I said.

The partner laughed.

"No shit," he said. And whacked me on the side of the left knee with the nightstick. The pain ran up and down the length of my leg.

"I'll help you think," he said. "Maybe you heard something, ah, government-related."

"Like what?" I said and he whacked my knee again and I felt the inside of my head get red, and, from a seated position, I punched him in the groin, which was about eye-level for me. He gasped and doubled over and staggered back. The nightstick clattered on the concrete floor. The deputies grabbed me. Vest lurched off the wall in a shooter's crouch with a small handgun. The partner stayed doubled over. I knew what he was doing; he was fighting off the nausea that came in waves.

"Cuff him," Vest said. His voice was raspy. "Cuff him to the bars."

The deputies hesitated. Vest stowed his gun, bent over and picked up the nightstick his partner had dropped.

"This ain't our deal," one of the deputies said. He was a beefy guy with sandy hair and freckled arms and a big, untrimmed moustache.

"Do what I tell you," Vest said. "This is a fucking federal matter."

"You say so," the deputy said. "But I ain't seen shit to prove it."

"You never hung nobody on a cell door before?" Vest said.

"Sure, but Sheriff don't much like us rousting white people 'less we have to."

"Fuck the Sheriff," Vest said.

"Sheriff don't too much like people saying fuck him, either."

"Okay," Vest said. "Okay. But this is important. National security. We have to find out what he knows. And we have to find out fast."

The partner had made it to the wall, and was leaning his forehead against it, trying to breathe deeply.

"You got the Sheriff's call, didn't you?" he said, wedging the words in between deep inhales. "It's on him, and us."

The deputy nodded, and looked at the other deputies, and shrugged. He put his nightstick under his left arm and took a pair of cuffs off the back of his belt.

"We got to do it," he said to me. "Hard or easy, up to you."

I said, "Hard, I think."

The deputy shrugged again, took the nightstick out from under his arm, and Martin Quirk walked into the cell. Everybody stopped in mid-motion and stared at him. He was as immaculate as always. Blue blazer, white Oxford button-down, maroon and navy rep striped tie, maroon show hankie, and gray covert slacks. He had his badge in his left hand. And he held it out so people could see it.

The partner had gotten himself upright, still breathing heavily, and turned so he was leaning his back on the wall.

"Who the fuck are you?" he said.

"Detective Lieutenant Martin Quirk, Commander, Homicide Division, Boston, Massachusetts, Police Department."

"We're in the middle of an investigation, Lieutenant," the partner said. "And, you know, this isn't Boston."

He had his breathing under control again, but he still leaned on the wall. And when he moved he did so stiffly. Quirk looked at him. There was something in Quirk's eyes. The way there was something in Hawk's. It wasn't just dangerous. I'd seen that look in a lot of eyes. It was more than that. It was a contemptuous certainty that if there was any reason to he'd kill you, and you had no part in the decision. Under all the tight control and the neat tailoring, and the pictures of his family on his desk, Quirk had a craziness in him that was terrifying when it peeked out. Here in the cellar of the Alton County Courthouse it not only peeked, it peered out, and steadily.

"I don't care what you shit kickers are doing," Quirk said, and what you saw in his look you could hear in his voice. "I want this guy, and I've come to get him."

Vest, who hadn't caught the look, and was too stupid to hear the sound in Quirk's voice, spoke while still looking at me.

"Hey, Lieutenant," he said. "Tough shit, huh? He's our prisoner and we are in the middle of interrogation. Whyn't you wait outside? Huh? Or maybe wait in Bahston."

Quirk stepped in front of Vest and put his face about an inch away from Vest's.

"You want to fuck around with me, dick breath?" Quirk said softly.

Vest stepped back as if something had pushed him. Quirk glanced around the cell.

"Before I came down here to this hog wallow, I talked with the U.S. Attorney in Boston, who put me in touch with the U.S. Attorney in Columbia. They both know I'm here."

He looked at me, and jerked his head.

"Let's go," he said.

"Certainly," I said.

And we walked unhurriedly out of the cell and down the corridor under the ugly ceiling lights and up some stairs and into the Alton County Sheriff's substation. Quirk demanded, and got, my personal stuff, including my gun, and we walked unhurriedly out onto the courthouse steps, where the sun was shining through the arching trees and the patterns of the heavy leaves were myriad and restless on the dusty street.

24

Quirk had parked his car in the fenced-in county lot back of the courthouse. We got in, and he pulled the car out the only exit, and parked on a hydrant across the street. He let the engine idle.

"How'd you get in there?" I said.

"Bullied the desk clerk," Quirk said.

"You're a scary bastard," I said.

"Lucky for you," Quirk said.

We were quiet.

"This a rental?" I said.

Quirk shook his head. "Federal guys in Columbia lent it to me."

"So why are we sitting here in it?"

"I thought we ought to see if we could get a read on the two suits in there," Quirk said. "I'd like to know who sent them."

From where we parked, we could see the front door of the courthouse and the parking lot entrance on the side street.

"We going to follow them?"

"Yeah."

"And they spot us?"

"They won't spot us," Quirk said. "I'm a

professional policeman."

"Sure," I said.

Quirk grinned.

"And if they do," he said, "fuck 'em."

Some cars came and went from the parking lot, but none of them contained Vest or the Partner. People went in and out of the courthouse, but they weren't ours.

"Why didn't you send Farrell?" I said.

"He's got some time off," Quirk said. "Trouble at home."

"What kind of trouble?"

"Guy he lives with has AIDS," Quirk said.

"Jesus," I said.

Quirk nodded, looking at the courthouse.

"How about him?" I said.

"He's okay," Quirk said.

"So you came because Farrell couldn't?"

"Right, and Belson's tracking down the other Olivia Nelson, or the real Olivia Nelson, or whoever the fuck that is in Nairobi, and the case is getting to be sort of a heavy issue . . . and I figure I better come down and save your ass, so Susan wouldn't be mad."

"Thanks," I said.

"You're welcome," Quirk said. "I called Hawk and he said he'd keep track of Susan until this thing shook down a little."

"You think someone might run at her to get to me?"

Quirk shrugged.

"Being careful does no harm," he said.

The two suits walked down the steps of the courthouse, came down the side street and into the parking lot. In a minute they exited the lot in a green Dodge, and passed us, and headed out Main Street. Quirk let his car into gear and followed them easily, letting several cars in between. Quirk was too far back to stay with them if the suits were trying to shake a tail. But they weren't. They had no reason to think they'd be followed. Quirk and I should be lickety-split for home. In ten minutes, they pulled into the parking lot of a Holiday Inn, out near the little airport, where Cessnas and Piper Cubs came and went several times a day, carrying Alton's heavy hitters to and from important events. Quirk and I dawdled in the parking lot of the Piggly Wiggly across the street, while the suits got out and went into the motel. Then we pulled over to the motel and parked. Quirk adjusted his gun onto the front of his belt so that it showed as he let his coat fall open. Then we went into the lobby and walked briskly to the desk clerk. Quirk flashed his badge, and put it away. It could have said *Baker Street Irregulars* on it, for all the clerk had a chance to read it.

"Lieutenant Quirk," he snapped, "Homicide. I need the room number of the two men who just came in here."

The desk clerk was a middle-aged woman with a lot of very blonde hair. She looked blank.

"Come on, Sis," Quirk said, "this is police business, I don't have a lot of time."

"The two gentlemen who just passed through here?"

Quirk looked at me.

"Is she a smart one?" he said. "Is this one a quick learner?"

He looked back at her.

"That's it, Sis. The two guys just passed through here. Room number and make it pretty quick."

He drummed on the counter softly with his finger tips.

"Yes, sir," the clerk said. "That would be Mr. O'Dell and Mr. Grimes. Room 211."

"Okay, we're going up," Quirk said. "If you do anything at all, except mind your own business, I'll close this dump down so tight it'll squeeze your fanny."

"Yes, sir," the clerk said. "Stairs at the end of the corridor, sir. Second floor."

"No shit," Quirk said, and turned and hustled down the corridor toward the stairs with me behind him.

"So tight," I said, "it'll squeeze your fanny?"

We were going up the stairs.

"Cops are supposed to talk like that," Quirk said.

"I liked 'The Killers' bit from Hemingway."

" 'Is she a smart one?' Yeah, I use that a lot."

We were on the second floor and stopped in front of room 211. Quirk put his ear to the door. He nodded to himself. Then he knocked on the door. There was a moment of silence, then the door half opened and Vest looked out. Quirk hit the door with his shoulder and Vest stumbled back. The door banged open wide.

The Partner was sitting on one of the twin beds with his back to the door, talking on the phone. He half turned as we came in and I kicked the door shut behind us.

He said, "What the fuck?"

Quirk walked over and broke the phone connection.

"Exactly," Quirk said.

A small holstered gun lay on top of the television set. Vest made a grab at it and yanked it from the holster. Quirk barely glanced at him while he chopped the gun out of Vest's hand and kicked it under the bed. Vest threw a punch at Quirk's head. Quirk slapped it aside and stepped away. He looked at me.

"You want this?" he said. "Even up the business in the jail?"

"Thank you very much," I said, and Quirk stepped behind me.

"All yours," he said, and I snapped a straight left out onto Vest's nose and drew blood. He put both hands to his face and took them away and stared for a moment at the blood on them. Noses bleed a lot. His partner moved toward me, in a low crouch, swaying gently, his hands up and close together. I turned slightly and drove my right foot in against his kneecap. His leg went out from under him and he fell over. Vest lunged toward the door and as he went past me, I hit him on the back of the head with my clubbed left forearm and he sprawled forward and banged his head on the door and slid to the ground. His partner was on his hands and knees now, scrambling toward the bed. I caught him and dragged him to his feet and turned my hip as he tried to knee me in the groin and took it on my thigh. I banged his nose with my forehead, and pushed him away and hit him left cross straight right, and he fell over on the bed and stayed there holding his nose, which had started to bleed as well. Vest was not unconscious on the floor, but he stayed there on his stomach with his face cradled in his arms.

"You guys are in trouble," Quirk said, "at several levels."

I glanced around the room. There was a wallet and a set of car keys on the night table beside the other twin bed.

"First of all, when you had enough help you were banging on a guy, with a billy."

I walked over to the night table and picked up the wallet. Nobody moved.

"Now you are alone, without backup, in a hotel room with the same guy, and look what happens."

I opened the wallet and looked at the driver's license. It was a Washington, D.C., license, issued to Reilly O'Dell. The Partner's picture was there, unsmiling. And a Georgetown address.

"That's one level," Quirk said. He ticked it off on his thumb. His voice was quiet, without anger, a little pedagogical, as if he were discussing evidence evaluation at the police academy, but tinged with sadness at the plight these men were in.

"Then there's the fact that this asshole" — he nodded at Vest on the floor — "told me to butt out and go back to Boston, and he made fun of my accent, by pronouncing it Bahston."

144

Quirk ticked that one off on his forefinger.

"I am, of course, en-fucking-raged," Quirk said. "Which is not good either, because I also can whup you to a frazzle."

Quirk smiled briefly and without humor at both of them, and held up a third finger. In Reilly O'Dell's wallet I found some business cards, with his name on them, and the name of his company, Stealth Security Consultants. I passed the license and one of the business cards to Quirk. Still holding his third finger up, in mid-count, he read them. And put them in his pocket.

"Third," he said. "You guys were participating in the illegal arrest and interrogation of a man whose constitutional rights you have violated worse than Sherman violated Atlanta. Fortunately, I happened by, and seeing an illegal injustice in progress, made a citizen's intervention. And now" — Quirk held up a fourth finger — "I discover that Mr. O'Dell, here, appears not even to be a police officer."

I bent over Vest and took the wallet from Vest's left hip pocket. I opened it and learned that his name was Edgar Grimes and that he too lived in Washington. And he, too, worked for Stealth Security Consultants. I gave his driver's license and one of his business cards to Quirk.

"Dandy," Quirk said. "Now, what the fuck is going on?"

Grimes had turned over on his back and sat on the floor, his back against the wall. His head was in his hands and he was rubbing his temples. The blood continued to run between his fingers and soak his shirt. O'Dell sat up stiffly on his bed not looking at anything. There was very little color in his face, and I could see his Adam's apple move as he swallowed. His nose seeped only a trickle of blood.

I went to the bathroom, put cold water on a face cloth, wrung it out, and handed it to Grimes on the floor. He held it against his nose.

"You can't stonewall," Quirk said. "You're down here representing somebody with enough clout to get the cooperation of the local Sheriff. Since you're from DeeCee, it's probably somebody in government. You've participated in a kidnapping. You've been caught by a policeman. We get the U.S. Attorney down here from Columbia with one phone call. We get the press down here with one other phone call. You people have fucked the duck, and your only chance to step out of it is to talk to me, frankly" — Quirk flashed the humorless smile again — "and openly."

I could hear both breathing, and then O'Dell sighed.

"You got a good argument," he said.

We waited.

The late morning sun beamed in through the east-facing bedroom window, and highlighted the dust motes, which drifted in and out of sight as they passed through the sunlight. The motel room was generic. Combination desk, dresser with a television set. A straight chair, two queen-sized beds separated by a table. A phone on the table, a lamp on the wall above it. The walls were beige, the rug was tan, there was an inexpensively framed print on the wall of some Anjou pears in a rose medallion bowl. The closet was behind a louvered door, the bath was past it. There was a brown Naugahyde armchair by the window. On top of the television set was a cardboard stand-up, which described the fun to be had in their lounge.

Grimes continued to hold the cloth against his nose. O'Dell sat up straight. His face was pale and scared; his wide, loose mouth seemed hard to manage.

"You used to work for the government," Quirk said. "Twenty years in, you took your pension and your contacts and set up in business for yourself."

"Yes," O'Dell said.

"And when you were a Fed," Quirk said, "you mostly spent your time subpoenaing records."

147

O'Dell started to protest and stopped and shrugged his high shoulders and nodded.

"You're in with tough guys, now," Quirk said.

O'Dell nodded. His hands were folded down at his paralleled thumbs, and he studied them, as if to make sure they were perfectly aligned.

"Your original question," O'Dell said.

Quirk nodded. Grimes's nose appeared to have stopped bleeding. But he continued to sit on the floor with his head in his hands.

"The thing is, we don't know what the fuck is going on."

"Tell me what you can," Quirk said. His voice was quiet.

Grimes's pale blond hair was thinning on top. With his head down, it showed the care with which he had combed his hair to hide that fact. The interchange with me had badly disarranged it, and, stiff with hair spray, the hair stood at random angles.

"We were told to come down here and try to get what he had found out about Olivia Nelson," O'Dell said.

Quirk smiled.

He said, "Un huh?"

"That's why we were kinda rough in the cell there," O'Dell said. "We didn't really know what to ask."

Quirk smiled understandingly.

148

"And you had four guys to help you," Quirk said.

O'Dell shrugged.

"Who asked you to find this out?" Quirk said.

"Mal Chapin."

"Short for Malcolm?" Quirk said.

"I guess."

"And who is Mal Chapin?" Quirk said.

O'Dell looked surprised. In his circles, Mal Chapin was probably an important name.

"Senator Stratton's office."

"He hired you?"

"Well, yeah. We're, like, ah, friends of the office, you know?"

"And the office steers business your way," Quirk said.

"Sure. That's how DeeCee works."

"Who arranged the deal with the Alton County Sheriff?"

"I don't know. I assume it was Mal. He's got a lot of clout with Party people around the country."

"And when you found out what Spenser knew," Quirk said, "what then?"

"We see if we can scare him off," O'Dell said.

"That'll be the day," I said.

I sounded exactly like John Wayne. No one

seemed to notice. Quirk looked at O'Dell for a long, silent moment. Then he took one of the business cards out of his pocket and went to the phone. He read the dialing instructions, and dialed.

"This is Lieutenant Martin Quirk," he said. "Is Reilly O'Dell there? . . . How about Edgar Grimes? . . . I'm the Homicide Commander, Boston Police Department. Please describe O'Dell for me."

He waited. Then he nodded.

"How about Grimes?" he said.

He waited some more.

Then he said, "No, Miss, that's fine. Just routine police business. What is your name, Miss? Thank you. No, they are not involved in a homicide."

He hung up.

"Your secretary is worried about you," he said.

Neither of them said anything.

"What is your secretary's first name?" Quirk said to O'Dell.

"Molly," O'Dell said.

"What's her last name?" Quirk said to Grimes.

"Burgin," Grimes said. He continued to hold his head in his hands and stare at the floor between his feet.

Quirk looked at me.

"Got any questions?" he said.

I shook my head.

"Okay," Quirk said.

We went to the door. Quirk paused and turned back to O'Dell and Grimes. A bruise was beginning to form on Grimes's forearm where Quirk had hacked the gun free.

"Have a nice day," Quirk said.

And we turned and left the room. Nobody said good-bye.

25

When Susan and I made love at her house, we had to shut Pearl the wonder dog out of the bedroom, because if we didn't, Pearl would attempt tirelessly to insinuate herself between us. Neither of us much wanted to leap up afterwards and let her in.

It was Sunday morning. We lay under one of Susan's linen sheets with Susan's head on my chest in the dead quiet house, listening to the sound of our breathing. I had my arm around her, and under the sheet she was resting the flat of her open hand lightly on my stomach.

"Hard abs," Susan said, "for a man of your years."

"Only one of many virtues," I said.

There was a big old wind-up Seth Thomas clock on Susan's bureau. It ticked solidly in the quiet.

"One of us has to get up and let the baby in," Susan said.

"Yes."

The sun was shining off and on through the tree tops outside Susan's bedroom window and the shadows it cast made small patterns on the far wall. They were inconstant patterns, disappearing when a cloud passed and reappearing with the sun.

"Hawk came by and took me to dinner while you were gone," Susan said.

"Uh huh."

"Fact, he came by several times," Susan said.

"He likes you," I said.

"And I swear I saw him outside my office a couple of times when I would walk a patient to the door."

"Okay, Quirk asked him to keep an eye on you when I got busted in South Carolina. He knew something was up and he didn't know what. Still doesn't."

"And Martin thought I'd be in danger?"

"He didn't know. He was being careful."

"So Hawk was there every day?"

"Or somebody, during the night too."

"Somebody?"

"Maybe Vinnie Morris, maybe Henry, maybe somebody I don't know."

"Maybe someone should have told me."

"Someone should have, but I'm the only one who knows how tough you are. They didn't want to scare you."

"And you think it's all right now?"

"Yeah. With Quirk involved, and the Federal Attorneys in Boston and Columbia. The cat's out of the bag, whatever cat it is. No point in trying to chase me away."

"So I don't need a guard?"

"No."

"Wasn't Vinnie Morris with Joe Broz?" Susan said.

"Yeah, but he quit him a while back, after Pearl and I were in the woods."

Susan nodded. We were quiet for another while. Susan moved the flat of her hand in small circles on my stomach.

"One of us has to get up and let the baby in," Susan said.

"Yes."

The mutable patterns on the far wall disappeared again, and I could hear a rhythmic spatter of rain against the window glass.

Susan said, "I'd do it, but I'm stark naked."

"I am too," I said.

"No, you're just naked," Susan said. "Men are used to walking around naked."

"Do you think stark naked is nakeder than naked?" I said.

"Absolutely," Susan said.

She tossed the sheet off of her.

"See?" she said.

I gazed at her stark nakedness for a while.

"Of course," I said and got up and opened the bedroom door.

Pearl rose in one movement from the rug outside the door and was on the bed in my place, with her head on my pillow, by the time I had closed the door and gotten back to the bed. I nudged her over a little with my hip and got in and wrestled my share of the sheet over me, and the three of us lay there with Pearl between us, on her stomach, her head on the pillow, her tail thumping, attempting to look at both of us simultaneously.

"Post-coital languor," I said.

"First," Susan said, "you tell me about South Carolina, and then we'll go out and have a nice brunch."

So I told her.

"And the woman in Nairobi really is Olivia Nelson?" Susan said.

"Yeah, guy from the American Embassy went over and talked with her. She's the real thing. Fingerprints all the way back to her time in the Peace Corps, passport, marriage certificate, all of that."

"Does she have any idea who the woman was that was killed?"

"Says no."

Pearl squirmed around between us until she got herself head down under the covers, and curled into an irregular ball, taking up much more than a third of the bed.

"What are you going to do now?" Susan said.

She had her hand stretched out above the bulge Pearl made in the sheet, and she was holding my hand, similarly stretched. The rain spattered sporadically on the windowpane, but didn't settle into a nice, steady rhythm.

"Talk to Farrell, report to Tripp, see what Quirk finds out."

"He's still in South Carolina?"

"Yeah, and Belson's going to go down. They'll talk with Jumper Jack, and with Jefferson, and they'll try to get a handle on Cheryl Anne Rankin."

"I'm glad you came back."

"Quirk and Belson will get further, they're official," I said.

"There was a time," Susan said, "when you'd have felt obliged to stay there and have a stare-down with the Sheriff's Department."

"I'm too mature for that," I said.

"It's nice to see," Susan said.

"But I will go back if I need to."

"Of course," Susan said. "Too much growth too soon would not be healthy."

"It's not just to prove I'm tough. The case may require it. I can't do what I do if I can be chased out of a place by someone."

Susan said, "A man who knows about such

things once told me, in effect, 'Anyone can be chased out of anyplace.' "

"Was this guy also a miracle worker in the sack?" I said.

"No," she said.

26

Farrell and I were in my office having some scotch from the office bottle. It was late afternoon, on Monday. Tripp was out of town. Senator Stratton's office had not returned my call.

"What do you know about Stratton?" I said. "Anything I don't?"

Farrell looked tired. He shook his head.

"Just what I read in the papers, and if you've ever been involved in something the papers wrote up, you know better than to trust them."

I nodded and dragged my phone closer and called Wayne Cosgrove at the *Globe*. He was in the office more now since they'd made him some sort of editor and he had a political column, with his picture at the top, that ran three days a week. When he answered, I punched up the speaker phone.

"You're on speaker phone, Wayne, and there's a cop with me named Lee Farrell, but all of this is unofficial and won't go any further."

"You speaking for Farrell, too?" Cosgrove said. He had a southern accent you could cut with a cotton hoe, although he'd left Mississippi at least thirty years ago, to come to Harvard on scholarship. I always assumed he kept the accent on purpose.

I looked at Farrell. He nodded. His eyes were red and seemed heavy, and his movements were slow.

"Yeah," I said. "Farrell too."

"Okay, pal, what do you need?"

"Talk to me about Senator Bob Stratton," I said.

"Ahh, yes," Cosgrove said. "Bobby Stratton. First off he's a pretty good Senator. Good staff, good preparation, comes down pretty much on the right side of most issues — which is to say I agree with his politics. Got a lot of clout, especially inside the Beltway."

"How about second off?" I said.

"Aside from being a pretty good Senator, he's a fucking creep."

"I hate it when the press is evasive," I said.

"Yeah. He drinks too much. He'd fuck a snake if you'd hold it for him. I don't think he steals, and I'm not even sure he's mean. But he's got too much power, and he has no sense of, ah, of limitation. He can do whatever he wants because he wants to and it's okay to do because he does it. He's the kind of guy who gooses waitresses. You understand?"

"Money?" I said.

"Yeah, sure. They all got money. How they get elected."

"Married?"

"To the girl on the wedding cake, two perfect children, a cocker spaniel, you know?"

"And a womanizer."

"You bet," Cosgrove said. "Far as I know, it's trophy hunting. I don't think he actually likes women at all."

"You know of any connection between him and Olivia Nelson, the woman who got killed couple of months back in Louisburg Square?"

"Loudon Tripp's wife," Cosgrove said.

"Un huh."

"I don't know any connection with her, but she's female — and Bobby is Bobby. Her husband probably knows Stratton."

"Why?"

"Because he's got money and contributes it to politicians."

"Democratic politicians?" I said.

"Politics makes strange bedfellows," Cosgrove said.

"I'd heard that," I said.

"Trust me, I'm a columnist," he said. "Why are you interested in Stratton?"

"Some people working for him tried to chase me off the Olivia Nelson case."

"Probably fucking her, and afraid it'll get out."

"Doesn't sound like the Olivia Nelson I've been sold, but say it was, and he was," I said. "Is it that big a secret?"

"He's probably going to be in the presidential primaries," Cosgrove said. "Remember Gary Hart?"

"Ah ha," I said.

"Ah ha?"

"You can say *strange bedfellows*, I can say *ah ha*."

"I thought the cops washed that case off," Cosgrove said. "Deranged slayer, random victim."

"You been punching the file up," I said, "while you're talking to me."

"Sure," Cosgrove said. "I haven't always been a fucking columnist. How come you're investigating?"

"Her husband wouldn't accept it. He hired me."

"You got a theory?"

"No."

"You make any progress?"

"No."

"Off the record?"

"No."

"So I tell you everything I know and you tell me shit," Cosgrove said.

"Yes."

We hung up.

Farrell and I looked at each other.

"You suppose she was sleeping with Stratton?" Farrell said.

I shrugged.

"I don't even know who she is," I said.

Farrell was silent. He nipped a little of the scotch. It was good scotch, Glenfiddich, single malt. We were drinking it in small measures from a couple of water glasses, which was all I had in the office. I was not fond of straight booze, but Glenfiddich was very tolerable.

"How is it at home?" I said.

"Home?"

"Quirk told me your lover is dying."

Farrell nodded.

"How soon?" I said.

"Sooner the better," Farrell said. "Final stages. Weighs about eighty pounds."

"He at home?"

Farrell shook his head.

"Hospice," he said.

His words were effortful. As if there weren't many left.

"How are you?" I said.

"I feel like shit," Farrell said.

I nodded. We both drank some scotch.

"You drinking much?" I said.

"Some."

"Any help?"

"Not much."

"Hard," I said.

Farrell looked up at me and his voice was flat.

"You got no fucking idea," he said.

"Probably not," I said.

"You got a girlfriend," he said. "Right?"

"Susan," I said.

"If she were dying people would feel bad for you."

"More than they would, probably, if she were a guy."

"You got that right," Farrell said.

"I know," I said. "Makes it harder. What's his name?"

"Brian. Why?"

"He ought to have a name," I said.

Farrell finished his scotch and leaned forward and took the bottle off the desk and poured another splash into the water glass.

"You can tell almost right away if people have a problem with it or not," he said. "You don't. You don't really care if I'm straight or gay, do you?"

"Got nothing to do with me," I said.

"Got nothing to do with lots of people, but they seem to think it does," Farrell said.

"Probably makes them feel important," I said. "You been tested?"

"Yeah. So far, I'm all right — we were pretty careful."

"Feel like a betrayal?" I said. "That you're not dying too?"

Farrell stared at the whiskey in the bottom of the glass. He swished it around a little, then took it all in a swallow.

"Yes," he said.

He poured some more scotch. I held out my glass and he poured a little in mine too. We sat quietly in the darkening room and sipped the whiskey.

"Can you work?" I said.

"Not much," he said.

"I don't blame you."

27

Hawk was skipping rope in the little boxing room that Henry Cimoli kept in the otherwise updated chrome and spandex palace that had begun some years back as the Harbor Health Club. It was a gesture to me and to Hawk, but mostly it was a gesture to the days when Henry had boxed people like Sandy Saddler and Willie Pep.

Now Henry had a Marketing Director, and a Fitness Director, and a Membership Coordinator, and an Accountant, and a Personal Manager, and the club looked sort of like Zsa Zsa Gabor's hair salon; but Henry still looked like a clenched fist, and he still kept the boxing room where only he and I and Hawk ever worked out.

"Every move a picture," I said.

Hawk did some variations, changed speeds a couple of times.

"Never seen an Irish guy could do this," he said.

"Racism," I said. "We never got the chance to dance for pennies."

Hawk grinned. He was working out in boxing shorts and high shoes. He was shirtless and his upper body and shaved head gleamed with sweat like polished onyx.

"Susan need watching anymore?"

"I don't think so," I said. "Who'd you use?"

"Me, mostly. Henry sat in once in a while, and Belson did one shift."

"Belson?"

Hawk nodded. From the rhythm of the rope, I knew that "Sweet Georgia Brown" was playing in the back of Hawk's head.

"She caught on," I said.

"Never thought she wasn't smart," Hawk said. "But I wasn't trying hard as I could."

"Know anything about the case?" I said.

"Nope, Quirk just called and said Susan needed minding."

I nodded and went to work on the heavy bag, circled it, keeping my head bobbing, punching in flurries — different combinations. It wasn't like the real thing. But it helped to groove the movements so that when you did the real thing, muscle memory took over. Hawk played various shuffle rhythms on the speed bag, and occasionally we would switch. Neither of us spoke, but when we switched, we did it in sync so that the patter of the speed bag never paused and the body bag combinations kept their pattern. We kept it up as long as we could and then sat in the

166

steam room and took a shower and went to Henry's office where there was beer in a refrigerator.

Henry was stocking Catamount Gold these days and I had a cap off a bottle, and my feet up. Hawk sat beside me, and I talked a little about the Olivia Nelson case. Through Henry's window, the surface of the harbor was slick, and the waves had a dark, glossy look to them. The ferry plowed through the waves from Rowe's Wharf, heading for Logan Airport.

"You know anything about Robert Stratton, the Senator?" I said.

"Nope."

Hawk was wearing jeans and cowboy boots and a white silk shirt. He had the big .44 magnum that he used tucked under his left arm in what appeared to be a snakeskin shoulder holster.

"Know anything about a woman named Olivia Nelson?" I said.

"Nope."

"Me either," I said.

"I was you," Hawk said, "and I had to go back down there to South Carolina, I'd talk to some of our black brothers and sisters. They work in the houses of a lotta white folks, see things, hear things, 'cause the white folks think they don't count."

"If they'll talk to me," I said.

"Just tell them you a white liberal from Boston. They be grateful for the chance," Hawk said.

"And, also, I'm a great Michael Jackson fan," I said.

Hawk looked at me for a long time.

He said, "Best keep that to yourself."

Then we both sat quietly, and drank beer, and looked at the evening settle in over the water.

28

The call was from Senator Stratton himself. It was ten-twenty in the morning, and the fall sun was warm on my back as it shone down Berkeley Street and slanted in through the window behind my desk.

"Bob Stratton," he said when I answered. "I think I've got some explaining to do to you, and I'd like to do it over lunch today if you're free."

"Sure," I said.

"Excellent. How about Grill 23, twelve-thirty. I'll book a table."

"Sure," I said.

"Just the two of us," Stratton said. "You and me, straight up, check?"

"Sure," I said.

"I'll have my driver pick you up," Stratton said.

"My office is two blocks from the restaurant," I said.

"My driver will stop by for you," Stratton said.

I said, "Sure."

"Looking forward to it," Stratton said.

We hung up. I dialed Quirk and didn't get him. I dialed Belson.

"Quirk back yet?" I said.

"Nope."

"You talk to him?"

"Yeah. The old black guy, Jefferson, doesn't say anything he didn't say to you. The old man doesn't say anything at all. Quirk agrees with you that Jefferson's lying about Cheryl Anne Rankin, but he can't shake him. The old lady at the track kitchen seems not to work there anymore. Nobody knows where she is. Nobody ever heard of Cheryl Anne Rankin. If he can't find the old lady from the track kitchen today, he's coming home. Travel money gives Command Staff hemorrhoids."

"Thanks," I said and hung up and sat and thought. Stratton had called me himself. That meant a couple of things. One, he wanted to impress me. Two, he didn't want other people to know that he had called or that we were lunching. So what did that mean? Why had Cheryl Anne's mother disappeared? Why would Jefferson, who was so forthcoming about everything else, lie about knowing Cheryl Rankin? Since Jumper Jack seemed to be his life's purpose, Jefferson probably was lying for him. Which meant that Jumper had something to do with Cheryl Anne.

I finished thinking because Stratton's driver

was knocking on my door. I didn't know anything I hadn't known before, but at least I didn't know less.

The driver was a polite guy with blow-dried hair, wearing a gray gabardine suit, and a pink silk tie.

"The Senator asked me to make sure you're not wearing a wire," he said. He seemed sorry about this, but duty-driven.

I stood and held my arms away from my sides. The driver went over me as if he'd done it before.

"May I look at the gun?" he said.

I held my jacket open so he could make sure it wasn't a recorder disguised as a 9mm Browning.

"Thanks," he said.

We went out to the Lincoln Town Car, which he had parked under a tow-zone sign. He held the back door open for me and I got in. Berkeley Street is one way the other way, so we had to go via Boylston, Arlington, Columbus, and back down Berkeley. I could have walked it in about a quarter of the time, but I wouldn't have been certified wire free.

Grill 23 is high-ceilinged and hard-floored. It is the noisiest restaurant in Boston, which is probably why Stratton chose it. It is hard to eavesdrop in Grill 23. The maitre d' managed to show me to Stratton's table without losing his poise. Stratton had a dark, half-drunk scotch and soda in front of him. He stood as I arrived, and put out a hand, made hard by a million handshakes. It was a politician's handshake, the kind where he grabs your hand with his fingers, no thumb, and spares himself squeezing. It was also damp.

"Bob Stratton," he said. "Nice to see you, nice to see you."

We sat. I ordered a beer. Stratton nodded toward his drink, which, from the color, was a double. Around us the room rattled with cutlery and china, and pulsed with conversation, none of which I could make out. For lunch the crowd was nearly all men. There was an occasional sleek female, normally lunching with three men, and one couple who were probably on vacation from St. Paul. But mostly it was men in conservative suits and loud ties.

"Well, how's the case going?" Stratton said. "Loudon Tripp is a fine man, and it was a real tragedy for him. You making any progress on running the sonovabitch to ground?"

It was a bright room, well lit, full of marble and polished brass and mahogany. Through Stratton's carefully combed and sprayed and blow-dried hair style, I could see the pale gleam of his scalp. His color was high. His movements were very quick, and he talked fast, so fast that, particularly in the noisy dining room, it took focus to understand him. I didn't answer.

The waiter returned with my beer and Stratton's scotch. It was a double, soda on the side. Stratton picked up the soda and splashed a little in on top of the whiskey.

"Gotta do this careful," he said, and smiled at me with at least fifty teeth, "don't want to bruise the scotch."

I nodded and took a sip of beer.

The waiter said, "Care for menus, gentlemen?"

Stratton waved him away.

"Little later," he said. "Stay on top of the drinks."

The waiter said, "Certainly, sir," and moved off.

Stratton took a long pull on his drink. There was a hint of sweat on his forehead. He looked at me over the rim of the glass like a man buying an overcoat.

"I've had my people check you out," Stratton said. "They tell me you're pretty good."

"Golly," I said.

"Tell me you are a very hard case, that you've got a lot of experience, and that you're smart."

"And a hell of a pistol shot," I said.

Stratton smiled because he knew I'd said something that called for it. I was pretty sure he didn't know what.

"Ever think of relocating?" he said.

"It's often suggested to me," I said.

"That a fact?" Stratton said. "I was thinking that there would be some real challenges for a man like you in Washington."

"Really?" I said.

"Absolutely," Stratton said. He drank most of the rest of his dark scotch, and his eyes began to look for the waiter. "Absolutely."

"That'd be great," I said. "I love those Puget Sound oysters."

The waiter spotted Stratton and came over, Stratton nodded toward the almost-empty glass. The waiter looked at me, I shook my head.

"What was that about oysters?" Stratton said.

"Nothing," I said. "I was amusing myself."

"You bet," Stratton said. "Anyway, I think I could help you to a pretty nice set up in Washington. You could be on staff, and still free-lance."

"Gee," I said.

The waiter returned with Stratton's double scotch — soda on the side. The open bottles of club soda were starting to pile up. Stratton paused long enough to splash in very little soda, from the newest bottle.

"So whaddya think?" he said.

I took a swallow of beer. It had gotten warm sitting there while Stratton inhaled his wine-dark scotch.

"I think you have your ass in a crack," I said.

Stratton laughed professionally. But his eyes seemed very small and cold and flat, like the eyes of some small predator. He put his scotch down carefully.

"You got to be kidding, my friend. You have got to be kidding. I have been in some tight places before, and I know a tight place when I see one. I mean, I've been a United States Senator for twenty-three years, and let me tell you something, I have faced down some hard moments."

"You sicked the Alton County Sheriff on me," I said.

Stratton started to speak and then stopped and sat back in his chair and stared at me.

"And a couple of ex-federal shoo-flys," I said. "And one of them hit me on the knee with a stick, and it's still sore. And you either tell me what your interest in the Olivia Nelson case is, or I am going to raise a great ruckus."

Stratton didn't move. I waited. A broad, charming smile spread across Stratton's face.

He let it rest there for a while for full effect.

"Well, by God, I guess my ass is in a crack, isn't it?" he said. "They were right about you; you are a guy doesn't miss a trick. Not a damned trick."

He laughed and shook his head. The waiter came over and asked if we'd care yet to order. Without looking at him, Stratton said, "Shrimp cocktail, steak rare, fries, a salad, house dressing."

"Very good, sir," the waiter said.

He turned to me. I ordered a chicken sandwich and a fresh beer.

"Would you care for another drink, Senator?" the waiter asked Stratton. Stratton shook his head and made a dismissive gesture with his hand. The waiter departed.

Stratton folded his hands and rested them on the edge of the table. He examined them for a moment after the waiter left. Then he raised his eyes and looked steadily at me, his face a mask of sincerity.

"Okay," he said. "Here's the deal. I was, ah . . ." He looked back at his knuckles. "I was . . ." He grinned at me, still sincere, but now a little roguish too. "I was fucking Olivia Nelson."

"How nice for her," I said.

"This is off the record, of course," Stratton said.

"Of course," I said.

"I got to know her at a few fund-raisers. Her husband's one of those Beacon Hill old money liberals, and one thing led to another, and we were in the sack."

Stratton winked at me.

"You know how those things go," he said.

"No," I said. "How?"

"Well, tell you the truth, it wasn't even my idea, I mean, Livvie was a hot item," Stratton said.

He leaned across the table toward me now, a couple of good old boys talking about conquests.

"You know there was the official version — great wife, perfect mother, charity, teaching, patron of the arts, all that public consumption bullshit. And Loudon, the poor, dumb bastard, probably believed it. He was one of those my-wife-this, my-wife-that guys, you know. Didn't have a clue, the dumb bastard. And every time there'd be a party or something, she'd pick out some guest and . . ." Stratton shrugged and spread his hands slightly.

"She was promiscuous," I said.

"The queen of the star fuckers," Stratton said. "You haven't had Livvie Nelson's pants off, you simply aren't important in this town."

"Always stars?" I said.

"Sure, it was like belonging to an exclusive club; you fucked Livvie Nelson, you knew you'd made it," Stratton said.

"Was it a long affair?"

"Not really an affair. It was great for a guy like me, just wham bam, thank you, ma'am. Usually she'd come to my office, when I was here in town. Very discreet. Nothing in public."

Stratton grinned at me again.

"I'm a married man," he said.

"I could tell," I said.

He shrugged and grinned at me further.

"And you were afraid," I said, "that my investigation would turn up this connection?"

"Exactly, my friend. Exactly right. At first, we thought you'd just go through the motions and take Loudon's money — he's got plenty. But then you went down there and we realized you were serious. And we figured maybe we lean on you down there, away from me, so there'd be no way to connect me to it, and off your home turf, you know, so you'd be a little more vulnerable? And we have a good friend in South Carolina, and he's holding some markers on the Alton County Sheriff . . ." He spread his hands again. "It's how things work."

"Who's the *we?*" I said.

"*We?* Oh, myself and my staff."

178

"So you went to all that trouble to keep me from finding out about you and Olivia Nelson."

"Yes. I told you, we had you checked out. We didn't like what we heard. You seemed to us like trouble and we wanted to get it under control right now."

"So your wife wouldn't know," I said.

"Well, Laura and I have a kind of understanding. But . . . we're planning for the presidential nomination, next time, maybe," Stratton said. "It could have hurt us."

"Still could," I said.

"Hey, this is off the record."

"What record?" I said. "You think this is an interview? I'm a detective. You could have killed her."

"Me?"

"You and your staff," I said.

"Don't be absurd," Stratton said. "I'm a United States Senator."

"I rest my case," I said.

29

Tripp's office was as peaceful as ever. Ann Summers was there at her desk, in a simple black dress today. She remembered me and was glad to see me, a combination I don't always get. On the other hand, given the activity level in the office, she was probably glad to see anyone.

"He's back," I said.

"Yes, he's just down the hall."

"Do you handle his checkbook?" I said.

"Mr. Tripp's? Not really, why do you ask?"

"His check bounced," I said and took the bank notice out of my pocket and showed it to her.

"Mr. Tripp's?"

"Un huh."

"Oh dear," she said.

"Probably a mistake," I said.

"Oh, I'm sure it is."

I waved it off and she showed me into Tripp's big office and sat me in the leather chair by his desk. The office was done in green. The walls and woodwork were green. The rug was a green Oriental, the furniture was cherry, the high-backed swivel chair behind Tripp's desk was cherry with green leather upholstery. The long desk had a red leather top, with a gold leaf design around the edges of it. There was a wet bar at the far end of the office, and a fireplace on the wall behind Tripp's desk. It was faced in a sort of plum-colored tile with a vine pattern running through the tiles, and it was framed on each side by big cherry book cases. The books looked neat and mostly unread. A lot of them were leather-bound to match the room. In two of the four corners there were cherry corner cabinets with ornate tops, and gold leaf dentil molding highlighting them. The corner cupboards were filled with designer knickknacks, and in the middle shelf on one of them was a picture of Olivia Nelson, or whoever the hell she had been, as a younger woman. Tripp's desktop was empty except for the onyx pen set, a telephone, and a big three-check checkbook. The checkbook was set square in the center of the desk as if to demand reconciling as soon as you sat down. I picked it up and opened the ledger pages, and ran back through them looking for my check. As I read, I noticed that there was no running balance. Each check was carefully entered, numbered and dated, but there was no way, looking at the checkbook, to know how much you had. I found my check, right below a check to Dr. Mildred Cockburn. I read back further. There were checks every month to Dr. Cockburn. All the entries were in the same thin hand. I'd seen it on my check. Most of the other checks were obvious. Telephone, electricity, insurance, cleaners, credit card payments. The only recurring one that was not obvious was Dr. Cockburn. Many of the check entries had *Returned* written across the original entry, in red ink, in the same hand, including several of Dr. Cockburn's. I looked a little harder. There seemed to be no checks rewritten to make good the ones that bounced. Something else was off in the check register. I didn't get it for a minute. I went back through more pages. And then I saw it. There were no deposits. In the whole ledger, there was no deposit entry. I put the checkbook back, and sat, and thought about that, and in a while, Tripp came into his office carrying a folded copy of *The Wall Street Journal*.

"Spenser," he said. "Good of you to come."

We shook hands, and he went around his desk and got into his padded leather swivel. He put the paper on the desk next to the checkbook, which he straightened automatically so that it was exactly square with the desk.

"Do you have a report for me?"

"Not exactly," I said. "Maybe a couple of more questions."

"Oh, certainly. But I am disappointed. I was hoping you'd have something."

I had something all right. But what the hell was it?

"Have you ever met any of your wife's family?" I said.

"No. She had none. That is, of course, she had one once, but they all died before I met her. She was quite alone, except for me."

"Ever been to Alton?" I said.

Tripp smiled sadly.

"No. There was never any reason."

I nodded. We were both silent for a moment.

"Sometimes," Tripp said, "I think I ought to go down there, walk around, look at the places where she walked, went to class, had friends."

He gazed past me, up toward the ceiling. Far below us, where State Street met Congress, there was traffic, and tourists looking at the marker for the Boston Massacre, and meter maids, and cabbies. Up here there was no hint of it. In Tripp's office you could just as well be in the high Himalayas for all the sound there was.

Tripp shook his head suddenly.

"But what would be the point?" he said.

There was something surrealistic about his grief. It was like a balloon untethered and wafted, aimless and disconnected, above the felt surface of life.

"How well do you know Senator Stratton?" I said.

"Bob's a dear friend. I've supported him for years. He was a good friend to Livvie as well, helped her get her teaching appointment, I'm sure. Though he never said a word about it."

"And you and your wife were on good terms?" I said.

Tripp stared at me as if I had offered to sell him a French postcard.

"You ask me that? You have been investigating her death for days and you could ask me that? We were closer than two people have ever been. I was she. She was I, we were the same thing. How could you . . . ?" Tripp shook his head. "I hope I've not been mistaken in you."

I plowed ahead.

"And you were intimate?"

Tripp stared at me some more. Then he got up suddenly, and walked to the window of his office, and looked down at the street. He didn't speak. I looked at his back for a while. Maybe I should investigate other career opportunities. Selling aluminum siding, say.

Or being a television preacher. Or child molesting. Or running for public office.

"Look, Mr. Tripp," I said. My voice sounded hoarse. "The thing is that stuff makes no sense. I know you're sad. But I've got to find things out. I've got to ask."

He didn't move.

"There's pretty good evidence, Mr. Tripp, that your wife's name is not, in fact, Olivia Nelson."

Nothing.

"That she was sleeping with Senator Stratton, and maybe with others."

Still nothing. Except his shoulders hunched slightly and his head began to shake slowly, back and forth, in metronomic denial.

"I've seen pictures of two different people both of whom look like your wife."

His head went back and forth. No. No. No.

"Have you ever heard of anyone named Cheryl Anne Rankin?"

No. No. No.

"Your retainer check bounced," I said.

The silence was so thick it seemed hard to breathe. Tripp's stillness had become implacable. I waited. Tripp stood, his head still negating. Back and forth, denying everything.

I got up and left.

30

Quirk and Farrell and Belson and I were in Quirk's office. Quirk told us that while he was in Alton he had learned exactly nothing.

"Everybody agrees that Olivia Nelson is married to a Kenyan citizen named Mano Kuanda and living in Nairobi. Embassy guy talked with her, took her fingerprints. We've compared them to her Peace Corps prints. She hasn't been in the United States since 1982. Never been in Boston. Has no idea who the victim is."

"She know anything about Cheryl Anne Rankin?" I said.

"No."

"Never heard the name?"

"No," Quirk said. "You talk to Stratton?"

"Yeah."

"And?"

"He says he was sleeping with Tripp's wife regularly, and that he wasn't the only one."

Quirk raised his eyebrows.

"Our Bobby?" he said.

"Shocking," Belson said. "And him a Senator and all."

"That's why he tried to chase you off?"

"So he says. Says he was afraid I'd find out about them and it would spoil his chances for the nomination next year."

"For President?" Quirk said.

"Yeah."

"Jesus," Belson said. "President Stratton."

"How about Tripp?"

"I talked to him."

"And?"

"He says everything was perfect."

"You got anything, Lee?" Quirk said.

Farrell jerked a little, as if he'd not been paying close attention.

"No, Lieutenant, no, I don't."

"Why should you be different?" Quirk said. He kept his eyes on Farrell for a long moment.

"One thing," I said. "I don't know why you would have, but has anyone run a credit check on Tripp?"

"Worried about your fee?" Belson said.

It was two-thirty in the afternoon and his thin face already sported a five o'clock shadow. He was one of those guys who looked clean-shaven for about an hour in the morning.

"In fact, his check bounced. But I think there's something goofy about his finances."

I told them about the checkbook.

"Might be something," I said.

"Lee?" Quirk said.

Farrell nodded.

"I'll find out," he said.

"Anything else?"

"The name Dr. Mildred Cockburn shows up in his checkbook a lot."

"Written like that?" Belson said.

I nodded.

"Probably not a medical doctor," Belson said.

"Yeah," I said, "then the check would be to Mildred Cockburn, DMD, or Mildred Cockburn, MD."

"Maybe she's a shrink," Belson said.

"Or a chiropractor, or a doctor of podiatry," I said.

"Hope for a shrink," Quirk said.

31

Susan and I had dinner at Michela's in Cambridge with Dennis and Nancy Upper. Susan knew Dennis from them both being shrinks. Nancy turned out to be an ex-dancer, so I was able to dazzle her with the knowledge of dance I had gained from Paul Giacomin, while Susan and Dennis talked about patients they had known.

I asked if either of them had heard of Dr. Mildred Cockburn. Neither of them had. Still, there was risotto with crab meat and a pistachio pesto. The room was elegant, and the bartender made the best martinis I'd ever drunk.

"I've got to find out how he does that," I said to Susan on the ride home.

"Well, you're a detective."

"And how complicated a recipe can it be?" I said.

"Vodka and vermouth?"

"Yeah."

"Sounds complicated to me," Susan said.

"Recipes are not the best thing you do," I said.

We were on Memorial Drive. Across the river the Boston skyline looked like a contrivance. The State House stood on its low hill, the downtown skyscrapers loomed behind it. And strung out along the flatness of the Back Bay, with the insurance towers in the background, the apartment houses were soft with the glow of lighted living rooms. It was Friday night. I was going to stay with Susan.

"Why do you want to know about Mildred Cockburn?" Susan said.

"Saw her name in Loudon Tripp's checkbook, 'Dr. Mildred Cockburn,' every month, checks for five hundred dollars. So I looked her up in the phone book. She's listed as a therapist with an office on Hilliard Street in Cambridge."

"Odd," Susan said.

"You'd expect to know her?"

"Yes."

"When I talk with her, what is it reasonable to expect her to tell me?" I said.

"Ethically?" Susan said.

"Yes."

"I can't say in the abstract," Susan said. "She should be guided by the best interests of her patient."

On our left, the surface of the river had a quick-silver gloss in the moonlight. A small cabin cruiser with its running lights on moved silently upstream, passing under the barrel-arched bridges, its wake a glassy furrow in the surface. Susan's street was silent, the buildings dark, the trees, half unleaved, made spectral by the street lamps shining through them.

Susan lived in an ornate Victorian house. On the first floor her office was on one side of the front hall, and her big waiting room was on the other. We went up the curving staircase to the second floor where she lived. When we opened the door, Pearl dashed at us, and jumped up, and tore Susan's hose, and lapped our faces, and ran to the couch and got a pillow and shook it violently until it was dead, and came back to show us.

"Cute," Susan said.

We took Pearl down and let her out into the fenced-in back yard. It was shadowy in the moonlight, but not dark, and we could watch her as she hurried about the yard, looking for the proper spot.

Later we lay in bed, the three of us, and talked, looking up at the ceiling in the moon-bright darkness. Pearl had little to say, but she compensated by taking up the most room in the bed.

"Is this Olivia Nelson thing making you crazy?" Susan said. We were holding hands under the covers, across Pearl's back.

"Nothing is turning out to be the way it appeared to be," I said.

"Things do that," Susan said.

"Wow," I said.

"I'm a graduate of Harvard University," Susan said.

32

Dr. Mildred Cockburn had office space in a tired-looking, brown-shingled house on Hilliard Street, down from the American Repertory Theater. There was a low wrought-iron fence with some rust spots around the yard. The fence had shifted over the years as the ground froze each winter and melted each spring, and it was now canted out toward the sidewalk. There was some grass in the yard, and a lot of hard-packed dirt. The front walk was brick, which had heaved with the fence. The bricks were skewed and weeds had grown up among them. Many of the brown shingles had cracked, and a couple had split on through, and the front door had been inadequately scraped before being painted over. Cambridge was not a hotbed of pretentious neatness.

A sign said *Enter*, which I did, and took a seat in a narrow foyer with doors leading out of it through each wall. I had an eleven o'clock appointment, and it was five of. The walls of the foyer were cream colored, though once they might have been white. There were a couple of travel posters on the walls, and an inexpensive print of one of Monet's paintings of his garden. There was also the insistent odor of cat. The low deal table beside the one straight chair had two recent copies of *Psychology Today*, and a copy of *The Chronicle of Higher Education* from last May.

At 11:06, the office door opened and a pale woman with a thin face, and her gray-streaked hair in a bun, came out of the office. She did not look at me. She took a long tweed coat from the coat rack, and put it on, and buttoned it carefully, and went out the door, maneuvering in the mailbox-sized foyer without ever acknowledging another presence.

There was a three- or four-minute wait thereafter, and then the office door opened again and Dr. Cockburn said, "Mr. Spenser?"

She wore a black turban and a large flowing black garment which I couldn't quite identify, something between a house coat and an open parachute. She was obviously heavy, though the extent of her garment left the exact heaviness in doubt. Her skin was pale. She wore a lot of eye makeup and no lipstick.

I stood, and she ushered me past her into the office. The office was draped in maroon fabric. The window had louvered blinds, opened over the top half, closed on the bottom. There was a Victorian sofa, upholstered in dark green velvet, against the wall to the right of the door, and a high-backed mahogany chair with ugly wooden arms, facing a wing chair upholstered in the same green. She sat across from me in the wing chair. She made a barely visible affirmative movement with her head, and then waited, her hands folded in her lap.

"This is not a therapeutic visit," I said. "I'm a private detective, and I've been employed by Loudon Tripp to investigate the murder of his wife, Olivia Nelson."

Again the barely visible nod.

"In the course of investigating, I came across your name."

Nod.

"I'm wondering if you could tell me anything about either of them," I said.

"That is unlikely," she said. She had a deep voice and she knew it. She liked having a deep voice.

"I realize," I said, "that there are questions of confidentiality here, but your patient's best interest might well be served by helping me find his wife's killer."

"Loudon Tripp is not my patient," she said.

Nothing moved when she spoke, except her lips. In her dark clothes and her deep stillness, she seemed theatrically inaccessible.

"Olivia Nelson," I said.

She remained motionless. I glanced around the room.

"You are a psychotherapist," I said.

Nod.

"Are you an M.D.?" I said.

She made the tiniest head shake.

"Ph.D.?"

Again, the tiny head shake.

"What?" I said.

"I am a Doctor of Human Arts."

"Of course," I said. "And the conferring institution?"

"University of the Southern Pacific."

"In L.A., I bet."

Nod.

"They give academic credit for life experience."

"That's quite enough, Mr. Spenser."

I nodded and smiled at her.

"Sure it is," I said. "So tell me about Olivia Nelson."

She paused for a long time. We both knew she was a fraud. And we both knew that if I were motivated, I could cause her a lot of aggravation with the state licensing board. And we both knew it. She shook her head ponderously.

"Troubled," she said, "terribly troubled."

I did a barely visible nod.

"And like a lot of women, terribly victimized," she said.

Her deep voice was slow. Her manner was ponderous. When she wasn't speaking, she remained entirely still. She knew I knew, but she wasn't letting down. She was going to stay in character.

I nodded.

"At the heart of things was the fact that her father rejected her."

"Original," I said.

"And so she sought him symbolically over and over in other men."

"She was promiscuous," I said.

"That is a masculine word. It is the product of masculine culture, judgmental and pejorative."

"Of course," I said.

"When she came to me for help, she had already tried the route of Freudian, which is to say, masculine, psychotherapy. The failure was predictable. I was able to offer her a feminist perspective. And understanding herself, for the first time, in that perspective, she began finally to get in touch with her stifled self, the woman-child within."

"And she slept around," I said.

"She gave herself permission to discover her sexuality. And to do so for its own sake, rather than in the service of a thwarted father love."

"Do you know the names of any other men she gave herself permission to discover her sexuality with?"

"Really, Mr. Spenser. That is privileged communication between patient and therapist."

"And one of them might have killed her," I said.

She chewed on that for a little bit.

"I would think it would be in her best interest for you to name them," I said. "I'll bet that in your studies at USP you learned that your patients' best interest was the ethical rule of thumb in difficult circumstances."

She chewed on that a little bit more.

"I don't make notes," she said finally. "I believe it inhibits the life force spontaneity necessary to a successful therapy."

"Of course," I said.

She allowed me to watch her think.

"And she never used names. She referred to the men in her life in various ways — the news anchor, for instance, and the judge, the broker, that sort of thing. There was an important clergyman, I know. But I don't know who he was."

"Denomination?" I said.

She shook her head. "Not even that," she said. "She always referred to him as the Holy Man. I think it pleased her to experience a man of the cloth."

I pressed her a little, but there was no more. I moved on.

"Did she tell you her real name?" I said.

"I was not aware that she had another," Cockburn said.

"What was her father's name?"

"I don't know. I had assumed it was Nelson."

"She ever mention the name Rankin?"

"No."

"Cheryl Anne?"

"No."

We were quiet. Dr. Cockburn maintained her ponderous certitude even in silence. The way she sat bespoke rectitude.

"She did say that she used another identity to get into graduate school, someone else's records and such," Cockburn said finally. "She herself had not finished high school. She left home at seventeen and went to Atlanta, and made a living as best she could, she said, including prostitution. At some point she came to Boston, motivated, I think, by some childhood impression of gentility, became a graduate student, made a point of frequenting the Harvard-MIT social events and met her current husband."

"She didn't say whose identity she used."

"No, but if in fact she is not Olivia Nelson, as you imply, then one might assume she used that one."

"One might," I said. "How did her father's rejection manifest itself?" I said.

"He failed entirely to acknowledge her."

"Tell me about that," I said. "How does that work? Did he pretend she wasn't there? Did he refuse to talk to her when she came home?"

Dr. Cockburn gazed ponderously at me. She let the silence linger, as if to underline her seriousness. Finally she spoke.

"He was not married to her mother. The lack of acknowledgement was literal."

I sat in the heavily draped room feeling like Newton must have when the apple hit him on the head. Dr. Cockburn looked at me with heavy satisfaction.

"Goddamn," I said.

"Was that all?" Susan asked later.

"Everything essential," I said. "I used my full fifty minutes, but the rest of it was just her doing Orson Welles."

We were having a drink at the Charles Hotel, which was an easy walk from Susan's home. Susan had developed a passion for warm peppered vodka, olives on the side. In an evening she would often polish off nearly half a glass.

"She did say that Olivia was obsessed with

money, and that apparently the family business was slipping."

"That would support the bounced check and the checkbook with no running balance," Susan said.

"Yeah. Cockburn said she had some sort of desperate plan, but Olivia wouldn't tell her what it was."

"Plan to get money?"

"Apparently. Cockburn doesn't know, or won't say."

"Dr. Cockburn has, in effect, waived her patient-therapist privilege already. I assume she'd have no reason to withhold that."

"Agreed," I said. "What do you think?"

"Dr. Cockburn's theory about Olivia Nelson is probably accurate. It doesn't require a great deal of psychological training to notice that many young people attempt to reclaim a parent's love by sleeping with surrogates. Often the objects of that claim are in some way authority figures."

"Like a U.S. Senator," I said.

"Sure," Susan said. "Sometimes it's apparent power like that, sometimes it's more indirect. Money maybe, or size and strength."

"Does this explain our relationship?" I said.

"No," Susan said. "Ours is based, I think, on undisguised lust."

"Only that?" I said.

"Yes," Susan said and guzzled half a gram of her peppered vodka. "I always wanted to boff a big goy."

"Anyone would," I said.

"Why," Susan said, "if she were sleeping with all these prominent men, would the police not discover it?"

"Partly because they were prominent," I said. "The affairs were adulterous, and prominent people don't wish to be implicated in adulterous affairs."

Susan was nodding her head.

"And because they were prominent," she said, "they had the wherewithal to keep the event covered up."

"She wasn't telling," I said, "and they weren't telling, and apparently they were discreet."

I shrugged, and spread my hands.

"What's a cop to do?" Susan said.

"Especially when the cop is being told by everyone involved that the victim was Little Mary Sunshine."

"So they weren't looking for infidelity," Susan said.

"Cops are simple people, and overworked. Most times the obvious answer is the right answer. Even, occasionally, when it's not the right answer, it's the easy one. Especially in a case like this where a lot of prominent people seem to be pushing you toward the easy answer."

"Even Martin?" Susan said.

"You can't push Quirk, but he's a career cop. It's his nationality — cop. If the chain of command limits him, he'll stay inside those limits."

"And not say so?"

"And not even think there are limits," I said.

"But he sent Loudon Tripp to you."

"There's that," I said.

"But could Tripp really have been so oblivious?" Susan said.

"And if he wasn't, why did he hire me?"

Susan sampled a bit of olive, and washed it down with a sip of peppered vodka. She seemed to like it.

"It is, as you know, one of the truisms of the shrink business that people are often several things at the same time. Yes, Tripp probably is as oblivious as it seems, and no, he wasn't. Part of him perhaps feared what the rest of him denied and he wanted to hire you to prove that she was what he needed to think she was."

"So, in effect, he didn't really hire me to find out who killed her. He hired me to prove she was perfect."

"Perhaps," Susan said.

"Perhaps?" I said. "Don't you shrinks ever say anything absolutely?"

"Certainly not," Susan said.

"So maybe the murder was the excuse, so to speak, for him to finally put his fears to rest, even if retrospectively."

Susan nodded.

"He would have a more pressing need, in fact, once she was dead," she said. "Because there was no chance to fix it, now. What it was, was all that he had left."

The bar was almost empty on a mid-week night. The waitress came by and took my empty glass and looked at me. I shook my head and she went away. The other couple in the bar got up. The man helped the woman on with her coat, and they went out. In the courtyard outside the hotel, a college-age couple went by holding hands, with their heads ducked into the wind.

"He doesn't want the truth," I said.

"Probably not," Susan said. "He has probably hired you to support his denial."

"Maybe he should get the truth anyway."

"Maybe," Susan said.

"Or maybe not?" I said.

"Hard to say in the abstract."

Susan smiled at me. There was compassion and intelligence in the smile, and sadness.

"On the other hand, you have to do what

you do, which may not be what he wants you to do."

I stared out at the courtyard some more. It was empty now, with a few dead leaves being tumbled along by the wind.

"Swell," I said.

33

Farrell came into my office in the late afternoon, after his shift.

"You got a drink?" he said.

I rinsed the glasses in the sink and got out the bottle and poured each of us a shot. I didn't really want one, but he looked like he needed someone to drink with. It was a small sacrifice.

"First we went back over Cheryl Anne Rankin again," Farrell said.

He held his whiskey in both hands, without drinking any.

"And we found nothing. No birth record, no public school record, no nothing. The woman who worked in the track kitchen is gone, all we got is that her name was Bertha. Nobody knows anything about her daughter. There's no picture there like you describe, just one picture of Olivia Nelson with a horse."

"Yeah," I said. "That was there too."

"Nobody remembers another one."

"Anyone talk to the black woman that worked there?"

"Yeah. Quirk talked with her while he was there. She doesn't know anything at all. She probably knows less than that talking to a white northern cop."

"Who's doing the rest of the investigating?"

"Alton County Sheriff's Department," Farrell said.

"You can count on them," I said.

Farrell shrugged.

"Per diem's scarce," he said.

He was still holding the whiskey in both hands. He had yet to drink any.

"You hit one out, though, on Tripp," he said. "He's in hock. First time around we weren't looking for it, and nobody volunteered. As far as we can find out this time, he has no cash, and his only assets are his home and automobile. He's got no more credit. He's a semester behind in tuition payments for each kid. His secretary hasn't been paid in three months. She stays because she's afraid to leave him alone."

"What happened?" I said.

"We don't know yet how he lost it, only that he did."

"How about the family business?"

"He's the family business. He managed the family stock portfolio. Apparently that's all he did. It took him maybe a couple hours, and he'd stay there all day, pretending like he's a regular business man."

"Secretary sure kept that to herself," I said.

"She was protecting him. When we showed her we knew anyway, she was easy. Hell, it was like a relief for her; she couldn't go on the rest of her life taking care of him for nothing."

"What's he say about this?"

"Denies everything absolutely," Farrell said. "In the face of computer printouts and sworn statements. Says it's preposterous."

"He's been denying a lot, I think."

Farrell nodded and looked down at the whiskey still held undrunk in his two hands. He raised the glass with both hands and dropped his head and drank some, and when he looked up there were tears running down his face.

"Brian?" I said.

Farrell nodded.

"He died," I said.

Farrell nodded again. He was struggling with his breathing.

"I'm sorry," I said.

Farrell drank the rest of his drink and put the glass down on the edge of the desk and buried his face in his hands. I sat quietly with him and didn't say anything. There wasn't anything to say.

34

Leonard Beale had an office in Exchange Place, a huge black glass skyscraper that had been built behind the dwarfed façade of the old Boston Stock Exchange on State Street. Keeping the façade had been trumpeted by the developer as a concern for preservation. It resulted in a vast tax break for him.

"Loudon lost almost everything in October 1987, when the market took a header," Beale said. "I wouldn't, under normal circumstances, speak so frankly about a client's situation. But Loudon . . ." Beale shook his head.

"He's in trouble, isn't he?" I said.

"Bad," Beale said. "And it's not just money."

"I didn't know brokers said things like 'it's not just money.' "

Beale grinned.

"Being a good broker is taking care of the whole client," he said. "It's a service business."

Beale was square-built and shiny with a clean bald head, and a good suit. He looked like he probably played a lot of hand ball.

"He lost his money in '87?" I said.

"Yeah. In truth, I didn't help. I was one of a lot of people who couldn't read the spin right. I didn't think the market was going to dive. But mostly he lost it through inattention. He always insisted on managing the money himself. Gave him something to do, I suppose. Let him go to the office at nine in the morning, come home at five in the afternoon, have a cocktail, dine with the family. You know? Like Norman Rockwell. But he wasn't much of a manager, and when the bottom fell out he was mostly on margin."

"And had to come up with the cash," I said.

"Yes."

"Why was he on margin?" I said. "I thought the Tripp fortune was exhaustive."

Beale shrugged and gazed out the window, across the Back Bay, toward the river. The sky was bright blue and patchy with white clouds. In the middle distance I could see Fenway Park, idiosyncratic, empty, and green.

"Are the Rockefellers on margin?" I said. "Harvard University?"

Beale's gaze came slowly back to me.

"None of them was married to Olivia," he said.

"She spent that much?"

"Somebody did. More than the capital generated."

"So he began to erode the capital," I said. Beale nodded.

"The first sure sign of disaster for rich people," he said. "Rich people don't earn money. Their capital earns money. If they start snacking on the capital, there's less income earned, and then, because they have less income, they take a bigger bite of capital, and there's even less income, and, like that."

"He tell you this?"

"No," Beale said. "He wouldn't say shit if he had a mouthful. As far as he was concerned, she was perfect. The kids were perfect. Christ, the son is an arrogant little thug, but Loudon acts like he's fucking Tom Sawyer. Buys the kid out of every consequence his behavior entails. Or did."

"And the daughter?"

"Don't know. No news is probably good news. Loudon never had much to say about her, so she probably didn't get in much trouble."

"And he's been economically strapped since 1987?"

"Broke," Beale said. "Getting broker."

"What are they living on?" I said. "They've got two kids in college, a mansion on the Hill, fancy office. How are they doing that?"

Beale shook his head.

"Margin," he said.

35

"It's simply not so," Loudon Tripp said.

"So why is everyone telling me otherwise?" I said.

"I can't imagine," Tripp said.

"Your secretary hasn't been paid her salary," I said.

"Of course she has."

He took his checkbook from its place on the left-hand corner of the desk and opened it up and showed me the neat entries for Ann Summers.

"And the check you gave me bounced," I said.

He turned immediately to the entry for my check.

"No," he said. "It's right here. Everything is quite in order."

"There's no running balance," I said.

"Everything is in order," Tripp said again.

"Do you know that your wife was unfaithful?" I said.

"By God, Spenser," he said, "that's enough."

His voice was full of sternness but empty of passion.

"I fear that I have made a mistake with you, and it is time to rectify it."

"Which means I'm fired," I said.

"I'm afraid so. I'm sorry. But you have brought it on yourself. You have made insupportable accusations. My wife may be dead, Mr. Spenser, but her memory is alive, and as long as I'm alive, no one will speak ill of her."

"Mr. Tripp," I said. "Your wife was not what she appeared to be, not even who she said she was. Your life is not what you say it is. There's something really wrong here."

"Good day, Mr. Spenser. Please send me a bill for your services through" — he looked at his watch — "through today," he said.

"And you'll pay it with a rubber check," I said. "And enter it carefully and not keep a balance so you won't have to know it's rubber."

"Good day, Mr. Spenser!"

I was at a loss. It was like talking to a section of the polar ice cap. I got up and went out, and closed the door behind me.

"He's crazy," I said to Ann Summers.

She shook her head sadly.

"Why didn't you tell me about him right off?"

"I don't know. He's, he's such a sweet man. And it seemed gradual, and he seemed so sure everything was all right, and . . ."

She spread her hands.

"Even when you weren't getting paid?" I said.

"I felt sorry, no, not that, quite, I felt . . . embarrassed, for him. I didn't want anyone to know. I didn't want him to know that I knew."

"Anything else you haven't told me?" I said.

She shook her head. We were quiet for a while. Then she spoke.

"What are you going to do?" she said.

"I'm going to find out," I said. "I'm going to keep tugging at my end of it until I find out."

She looked at me for a long time. I didn't have anything to say. Neither did she. Finally she nodded slowly. In its solemnity, her face was quite beautiful.

"Yes," she said. "You will, won't you."

36

Williams College was located in Williamstown, in the far northwest corner of Massachusetts. The ride out was more than three hours whether you went on the Mass. Pike or Route 2. On the one hand, if you got behind some tourist in the two-lane stretches of Route 2, the trip became interminable. On the other hand, Route 2 was better-looking than the Mass. Pike and there was not a single Roy Rogers restaurant the whole way.

Susan and I had a reservation in Williamstown at a place called The Orchards where they served home-baked pie, and we could have a fire in the bedroom. While I talked with the Tripp children, Susan would visit the Clark Museum.

We drove out on Route 2. Susan had a new car, one of those Japanese things she favored that were shaped like a parsnip, and mostly engine. This one was green. She let me drive, which was good. When she drove, I tended to squeeze my eyes tight shut in terror, which would cause me to miss most of the scenery that we had taken Route 2 to see in the first place.

I met Chip and Meredith Tripp in the bar of a restaurant called the River House, which, in the middle of the day, was nearly empty. Chip and I each had a beer. Meredith had a diet Coke. Chip was cooler than kiwi sorbet, with his baggy pants, and purple Williams warm-up jacket, his hat on backwards, and his green sunglasses hanging around his neck. Meredith was in a plaid skirt and black turtleneck and cowboy boots. As always she had on too much makeup.

"I need to talk with you about your mother," I said.

Chip glowered. Meredith looked carefully at the table top.

"What I will tell you can be confirmed in most of its particulars, by the police. So we shouldn't waste a lot of time arguing about whether what I say is true."

"So you say, Peeper."

Peeper. I took a deep breath and began.

"First of all, it is almost certain that your mother was not in fact Olivia Nelson."

Meredith's eyes refocused on the wall past my chair and got very wide.

Her brother said, "You're full of shit."

"Did either of you ever meet any of your mother's family?"

"They're dead, asshole," Chip said. "How

216

are we going to meet them?"

I inhaled again, slowly.

"I'll take that as no," I said and looked at Meredith. She nodded, her head down.

"Have you ever heard of anyone named Cheryl Anne Rankin?"

Chip just stared at me. Meredith shook her head.

"Do you know that your father is encountering financial difficulty?" I said.

"Like what?" Chip said.

"He's broke," I said.

"Bullshit," Chip said.

I nodded slowly for a minute, and inhaled carefully again.

"Did you know that your mother was promiscuous?" I said.

"You son of a bitch," Chip said.

He stood up.

"On your feet," he said.

I didn't move.

"Hard to hear," I said. "I don't blame you. But it has to be contemplated."

"Are you gonna stand up, you yellow bastard, or am I going to have to drag you out of your chair?"

"Don't touch me," I said.

And Chip heard something in my voice. It made him hesitate.

I tried to keep my voice steady.

"I am going to find out how your mother died, and the only way I can is to keep going around and asking people questions. Often they don't like it. I'm used to that. I do it anyway. Sometimes they get mad and want to fight me, like you."

I paused and kept my eyes on his.

"That's a mistake," I said.

"You think so," he said.

"You're an amateur wrestler," I said. "I'm a professional thug."

Meredith put her hand on Chip's arm, without looking at him.

"Come on, Chip," she said. There was almost no affect in her voice.

"I'm not going to sit around and let him talk about her that way."

"Please, Chip. Let him . . ." Her voice trailed away.

I waited. He glared at me for a moment, then slammed his chair in against the table.

"Fuck you," he said to me and turned and left.

Meredith and I were quiet. She made an embarrassed laugh, though there was nothing funny.

"Chippy's so bogus, sometimes," she said.

I waited. She laughed again, an extraneous laugh, something to punctuate the silence.

"You know about your mother?" I said.

218

"Dr. Faye says we all do and won't admit it. Not about her being somebody else, but the other . . ."

I nodded.

"Daddy would be up in his room with the TV on," Meredith said in her small flat voice. "Chip was at college. And she would come home; I could tell she'd been drinking. Her lipstick would be a little bit smeared, maybe, and her mouth would have that sort of red chapped look around it, the way it gets after people have been kissing. And I would say, 'You're having an affair.' "

"And?"

"And she would say, 'Don't ask me that.' "

"And I would say, 'Don't lie to me.' "

I leaned forward a little trying to hear her. She had her hands folded tightly in front of her on the table top and her eyes were fastened on them.

"And her eyes would get teary and she would shake her head. And she'd say, 'Oh, Mere, you're so young.' And she would shake her head and cry without, you know, boo-hooing, just talking with the tears running down her face, and she'd say something about 'life is probably a lie,' and then she'd put her arms around me and hug me and pat my hair and cry some more."

"Hard on you."

"When I came to school," she said, "I was having trouble, you know, adjusting. And I talked with Jane Burgess, my advisor, and she got me an appointment with Dr. Faye."

"He's a psychiatrist?"

"Yes." The word was almost nonexistent, squeezed out in the smallest of voices. Her Barbie doll face, devoid of character lines, showed no sign of the adult struggle she was waging. It remained placid, hidden behind the affectless makeup.

"Know anything about money?" I said.

"Sometimes they'd fight. She said if he couldn't get money, she would. She knew where to get some."

"What did he say?"

"Nothing. He'd just go upstairs and turn on the television."

"What would she say?"

"She'd go out."

"You don't know what her plan was? For money?"

"She always just said she knew where to get it."

"How long did you live like this?"

"I don't know. All the time, I guess. Dr. Faye says I didn't buy the family myth."

I put a hand out and patted her folded fists. She got very rigid when I did that, but she didn't pull away.

"Stick with Dr. Faye," I said. "I'll work on the other stuff."

Susan and I were in the dining room at The Orchards, Susan wearing tight black pants and a plaid jacket, her eyes clear, her makeup perfect.

"There's a beard burn on your chin," I said.

"Perhaps if you were to shave more carefully," Susan said.

"You didn't give me time," I said. "Besides, there are many people who would consider it a badge of honor."

"Name two," Susan said.

"Don't be so literal," I said.

There were fresh rolls in the bread basket, and the waitress had promised to find me a piece of pie for breakfast. We were at a window by the terrace and the sun washed in across our linen table cloth. I drank some coffee.

"It is a lot better," I said, "to be you and me than to be most people."

Susan smiled.

"Yes, it is," she said. "Especially better than being one of the Tripps."

"What I don't get is the girl, Meredith. How did she escape it? She's very odd. She's obviously in trouble. Most of the time she's barely there at all. But she's the one that will look at it, that doesn't buy the family myth."

"There's too much you don't know," Susan said.

"I may have that printed on my business cards," I said.

The waitress appeared with a wedge of blackberry pie, and a piece of cheddar cheese beside it.

"My father used to have mince pie for breakfast," the waitress said, "almost every Sunday morning."

"And sired beautiful daughters," I said.

The waitress smiled and poured me some more coffee, and gave Susan a new pot of hot water, and went off. Susan watched me eat the pie. She was having All Bran for breakfast, and a cup of hot water with lemon.

"What will you do," Susan said, "now that you're fired?"

"I'll probably go back down to Alton," I said. "And ask around some more."

"Will it be dangerous?"

"Probably not," I said. "Most of the cat is out of the bag, by now. There's not much reason to try and run me off."

"You think Alton is where you'll find out?"

"I don't know," I said. "I don't know where else to look."

37

I was in the detectives' room at the Alton County Sheriff's Department talking with the pretty good-looking female cop who'd harassed me before. Her name was Felicia Boudreau, and she was a detective second grade.

"I didn't much like that deal," she said. "But you've been a cop. Do a lot of stuff you don't much like."

"Why I'm no longer a cop," I said.

She shrugged.

"You know who put us on you in the first place?"

I nodded.

"Senator Robert Stratton," I said.

"From Massachusetts?"

"That's the one," I said. "At least I never voted for him."

"What was his problem?" she said.

"I'm investigating a murder," I said. "Stratton was sleeping with the victim."

"Afraid you'd turn up his name?"

"Yeah."

"So what," she said. "That's mostly what

they do in the Senate, isn't it? They get laid?"

"He wants to be President," I said.

"Sure," she said. "Give him a fancier place to get laid in."

"Who put the tail on me?" I said.

She shook her head. She was sitting with her feet on the desk, crossed at the ankle. It showed a long, smooth thigh line. She had on light-gray slacks over black boots, and a flowered blouse with big sleeves. Her holstered gun, some sort of 9mm, lay on the desk beside her purse. Everybody had nines now.

"You grow up here in Alton?" I said.

"Yes."

"You know Olivia Nelson?"

"Jumper Jack's girl," Felicia said.

"Yes. Tell me about her."

"What's to tell. Rich kid, about ten years older than me. Father's a town legend, hell, maybe a county legend. Big house, race horses, good schools, servants, hunting dogs, bourbon and branch water."

"What happened to her?"

Felicia grinned.

"Town scandal," she said. "Went in the Peace Corps. Married some African prince with tribal scars on his face. Jumper never got over it."

"How about her mother?" I said.

"Her mother?"

"Yeah, everyone talks about Jumper Jack. I never hear anything about her mother."

"She had one," Felicia said.

"Good to know," I said.

"Sort of genteel, I guess you'd say. Sort of elegant woman who didn't like the muddy dogs in her house, and hated it that a lot of the time her husband would have horse shit on his boots at supper."

"That's genteel," I said.

"Yeah, it's hard to describe. But she was always like someone who thought she should have been living in Paris, reading whoever they read in Paris."

"Proust," I said.

"Sure."

"What happened to her?" I said.

"Committed suicide."

"When?"

"I investigated it. Lemme see, nineteen . . . and eighty-seven, late in the year. Almost Christmas. I remember we were working overtime on the sucker just before the holidays."

"1987," I said.

"Yeah. That mean something to you?"

"Year the market crashed," I said. "October 1987."

"You think she killed herself 'cause the stock market crashed?"

I shook my head.

"Doesn't sound the type," I said. "Know why she did it?"

"No. Went in her room, took enough sleeping pills to do the trick, and drank white wine until they worked. Didn't leave a note, but there was no reason to think that it wasn't what it looked like."

She got up and got two cups of coffee from the automatic maker on the file cabinet. She added some Cremora and sugar, asked me what I took, and put some of the same in mine. Then she brought the cups back to her desk and handed me one. The gray slacks fit very smoothly when she walked.

"How about Cheryl Anne Rankin?" I said.

"Your Lieutenant, what's his name?"

"Quirk."

"Yeah, your Lieutenant Quirk asked around about her. I don't remember her."

"He talk with you?"

"Nope. Sheriff said we was to stay away from him. Nobody would much talk with him."

"How come you're talking to me?"

"Sheriff didn't say nothing about you. Probably didn't think you'd have the balls to come back."

"There was a picture on the wall of the track kitchen," I said. "Looked like Olivia Nelson. Woman who worked there said it was Cheryl

Anne Rankin, and she was her mother. Now the picture's gone, and the woman's gone."

"Don't know much about that," Felicia said. "People work at the track kitchen come and go. They get paid by the hour, no real job record, nobody keeps track. If you can fry stuff in grease, you're hired."

"If you were trying to find out things in this town, who would you go to?"

"About this Cheryl Anne?"

"About anything, Cheryl Anne, Olivia, Jack, his wife, Bob Stratton, anything. The only thing I know for sure down here is that you get your hair done in Batesburg."

"And it looks great," she said.

"And it looks great."

We both drank a little of the coffee, which was brutally bad.

"Friend of mine said I might talk to the household help," I said. "They're in all the houses, all the offices. They're cleaning up just outside of all the doors, and they tell each other."

Felicia took another drink of the wretched coffee and made a face.

"I've tried," she said. "No point to it, they wouldn't tell me anything, just like they won't tell you. They'll listen politely and say 'yassah' and nod and smile and tell you nothing."

"I'm used to it," I said. "All races, creeds, and colors refuse to tell me stuff."

"And when they do, it's a lie," she said.

"That especially," I said.

38

There was no picture of Cheryl Anne Rankin in the track kitchen. The white woman who'd claimed her wasn't there either, though the black woman I'd seen before was still there. She didn't know where the white woman was. Nawsir, she didn't know her name. Never did know it. She didn't know nothing about no picture. Yessir. Sorry, sir. Take a walk, sir.

I went back to the Alton Arms and sat on the front steps. The Blue Tick hound that I'd seen on my last visit was stretched out in the sun on the front walk. He rolled his eyes back toward me, and looked at me silently as I sat down. I nodded at him. His tail stirred briefly.

"Contain yourself," I said.

Across the street a couple of jays were darting about in the branches of one of the old trees. While I watched them, I put my closed fist down toward the Blue Tick hound. Without raising his head, he sniffed thoughtfully. Then he stood up suddenly and put his head on my leg. I scratched his ear. He wagged his tail slowly. Behind me the door of the hotel opened and a fat gray-haired couple came out.

Sedale came behind them with four pieces of matched luggage. He stored the luggage in the trunk of a silver Mercedes sedan, accepted some change from the husband, and held the door while his wife hove herself into the passenger seat.

"Y'all have a nice day now, y'hear?" he said.

Then he closed the door and smiled at them. As they drove away, he tucked the change into his vest pocket.

"High rollers," I said.

The Blue Tick kept his head on my leg, and I continued to scratch his ear. Sedale smiled at me.

"How're you today, sir?" he said.

"You got a minute to sit here on the steps and talk to me?" I said.

"Don't like me to sit on the steps," Sedale said. "But I can stand here while you sit."

"They don't mind if I sit on the steps?" I said.

"You a guest, sir," Sedale said.

The dog left me and went to Sedale. He put his hand down absently, the way owners do, and the dog lapped it.

"I'm a detective," I said.

"I know that, sir."

"Be hard to prove given what I've detected so far," I said.

"Probably a very difficult case, sir."

The dog returned to me for more ear scratching.

"What do you know about me?" I said.

"Know you a private detective, down from Boston, looking into a murder. Mr. Jack Nelson's daughter."

"Un huh."

" 'Cept she ain't Mr. Nelson's daughter."

"You know Jefferson?" I said. "Works for Mr. Nelson."

Sedale smiled.

I stopped scratching the dog's ear as I talked and he tossed his head against my hand.

"Sorry," I said to the dog and scratched some more. "I saw a picture on the wall of the track kitchen of a young woman who looked just like Olivia Nelson had looked at that age. The woman at the track kitchen said her name was Cheryl Anne Rankin and that she was the woman's daughter. Now the picture's gone, and the woman's gone."

Sedale smiled encouragingly.

"You know anything about Cheryl Anne Rankin?" I said.

"Nawsir."

I nodded.

"The thing is, Sedale, that it is too big a coincidence that there should be two people look like Olivia Nelson in town, and then find twenty years later that one of them has disappeared and someone is impersonating the other."

"Yessir."

"And since we know that the real Olivia Nelson is alive in Africa, it seems to me that the dead woman has to be Cheryl Anne Rankin."

Sedale's face was inert. He showed no sign of impatience or discomfort. I had no sense that he wanted to leave. He had simply gone inside; placid, agreeable, and entirely unavailable to a white guy asking questions about a white matter. He nodded.

"I want to find out who killed her."

Sedale nodded again.

"Tell me about Cheryl Anne Rankin." I said.

"Don't know nothing 'bout that, sir," he said.

"The hell you don't," I said. "Jefferson knows something about her, so do you. But you duck into black face the minute I ask you. Until five minutes ago, you were an actual person. Then I started to ask about Cheryl Anne Rankin, and you turned into Stepin Fetchit. Your accent even got thicker."

"Yessir," Sedale said and grinned.

We were both silent. I continued to scratch the dog's ear. The dog continued to wag his tail. Sedale continued to rest his hips on the railing of the veranda. Then he reached into his vest pocket with two fingers and brought out a quarter and three dimes. He held them in the palm of his hand and showed them to me.

"See what those fatso tourists gave me for a tip?" he said.

"Let the good times roll," I said.

Sedale grinned suddenly.

"You ain't as fucking stupid as most honkies," he said.

"And your dog likes me," I said.

"For a fact," Sedale said.

He looked at his watch.

"I get off in an hour. You buy me couple of drinks at the Hunt Grill on Elm Street, I'll tell you 'bout Cheryl Anne Rankin."

39

I was the only white person in the Hunt Grill. No one appeared to care much about that fact, couple of heads turned and at least one guy nudged another, but mostly people were interested in their drinks and watching *Jeopardy*. The room was done in pine paneling. There were pictures of athletes on the walls, and sports pennants, and schedules of televised games. There were two very big-screen television sets, and a big sign advertising Happy Hour, which, according to the sign, I was in.

The bartender nodded at me when I squeezed onto a bar stool. I ordered a beer and got it. His dark eyes were without expression. His face held neither hostility nor welcome. He put a bowl of peanuts on the bar in front of me and moved away. I picked up a peanut and ate it carefully. No need for a whole handful. One at a time was just as succulent. I sipped a little of the beer. I picked up two peanuts. Everyone on *Jeopardy* was having a hell of a time. Just like me. I drank a little more beer. I took a handful of peanuts and munched them vigorously.

Sedale came in and walked toward me. The Blue Tick hound was with him. The bar was nearly full, but there was an empty stool on either side of me. Sedale sat on one. The hound sat on the floor near his feet.

"Seven and seven," he said to the bartender.

"Do you like that?" I said. "Or do you just order it because you like the way it sounds?"

The bartender put the drink in front of him and Sedale drank half of it.

"You know the difference between a toilet seat and a hotel worker?" Sedale said.

"No, I don't."

"Toilet seat only services one asshole at a time."

He drank the rest of his drink and gestured another at the bartender.

"His tab," Sedale said and jerked his head at me. The bartender looked at me. I nodded.

Sedale took a handful of peanuts and ate some and gave a couple to the dog. The bartender brought him his drink.

"My aunt Hester, my momma's oldest sister, she a midwife. Been a midwife fifty-something years. She a lot older than my momma," Sedale said.

He paused and sipped his second drink.

"Woman named Bertha Voss come to my aunt Hester 'bout forty years ago, little longer, and ask could she do an abortion for her."

The dog sitting on the floor had his nose trained on the peanuts. I took a couple, and held them down in the palm of my open hand, and he scarfed them off.

"Bertha was a no-account cracker. But she was white. Those days black people get lynched for things like that. My aunt Hester say, 'No, you got to find somebody else, or you got to have the baby.' "

Sedale sipped again. He took in his second drink quite delicately, holding the glass in his finger tips. The first one had been need. The second appeared to be pleasure. I finished my beer. The bartender looked over and I pointed at my glass. He brought a fresh beer and another bowl of peanuts. The first bowl had somehow emptied. Must have fed the dog too many.

"Well, Bertha couldn't find nobody, I guess, 'cause she married another no-account cracker name Hilly Rankin, and she had the baby. And she tell everybody it's his."

"Cheryl Anne?" I said.

"Yes, sir," Sedale said and there was a gleam of mockery in his eyes.

"Rankin believe he's the father?"

"Seemed to. Hilly ain't very smart."

"And do we know who the proud poppa was?"

"Sho 'nuff do," he said. "Care to guess?"

Sedale grinned at me like he was the host of *Jeopardy*. He let the pregnant pause hang between us.

"Jack Nelson," I said.

Sedale's grin widened.

"You a by-God real live detective, ain't you," he said. "Bertha told my aunt Hester that it was Jumper Jack knocked her up."

The Blue Tick hound nudged his head under my hand and stared at the bowl of peanuts. I gave him some. On the big screen television, Jeopardy had ended and the local news was on. It looked and sounded exactly like local news everywhere: a serious-looking anchor; an attractive, though not frivolous, anchorette; a twit to do the weather; and a brash guy that talked fast to do sports.

"You know where Bertha Rankin is now?" I said.

"Sure."

Our voices sounded hollow to me. As if they weren't connected to humans.

"Where?"

"She and Hilly got a dump out on the Batesburg Road 'bout five miles. Right past the gravel pit, dirt road goes down on the right. They at the end of it."

"You know Cheryl Anne?" I said.

"Nope. She musta gone to school in Batesburg."

"They kept it a secret," I said. "All this time."

"Sure," Sedale said. "Only the niggers knew."

"And now she's dead," I said.

It was one of those things you know for a long time before you know it. The dead woman in Boston was Cheryl Anne Rankin.

40

The weather in Alton was still warm and it didn't seem like fall. But at quarter to seven in the evening it was dark on the Batesburg Road. And empty, as if no one wanted to go to Batesburg, even to have their hair done. On the other hand, maybe no one wanted to leave Batesburg and go to Alton. I would have preferred neither.

I passed the gravel pit and turned right onto the dirt road and bumped slowly down to the end of it. My headlights hit on a cinder-block shack with a corrugated metal roof that looked like it might once have been used to house tractors. Someone had filled in the big garage-type doors with odd pieces of unpainted plywood, and cut a person-sized door in the middle of one of them. The door hung on badly nailed galvanized strap hinges, and opened with a rope pull. There was the rusted hulk of what might have once been a 1959 Plymouth in the yard, and several old tires. A dirty white sow lying behind one of the tires raised her head and stared into my headlights. I got out and knocked on the front door and the woman from the track kitchen opened it. She peered at me, trying to see into the darkness.

"My name is Spenser," I said. "We met once at the track kitchen."

She flinched back as if I had pushed her and glanced over her shoulder.

"I don't know you," she said.

"Yeah, you do. And I know you. You're Bertha Rankin, formerly Bertha Voss. You have a daughter Cheryl. Where's your husband?"

"He's asleep," she said, and glanced back into the room again.

I could smell bacon grease and kerosene and a strong reek of whiskey.

"We need to talk about Jack Nelson," I said. "If you'd like to step outside."

She hesitated, and then stepped out of the house and pulled the makeshift door closed behind her. She was wearing some sort of shapeless dress, over some sort of shapeless body. Her gray hair was down and lank, and her face was red. There was sweat on her forehead and I could smell whiskey on her too.

"What you want?"

"I know that Jack Nelson is the father of your daughter, Cheryl Anne Rankin. I have no need to tell other people about that, right now. But I need to talk with you about it."

"How you know that?" she said.

"Doesn't matter. Tell me when Cheryl Anne was born."

"1948."

"Same year as Olivia Nelson," I said.

Bertha Rankin didn't speak.

"Did she look like Olivia Nelson?"

Bertha Rankin nodded.

"Where did she go to school?" I said.

"Batesburg."

"Her father know about her?"

"Yes."

"He give you money?"

We were standing in my headlights. As if on stage. She looked at me and then back at the house and then at the ground.

"Just you and me," I said. "Did Jack Nelson give you money?"

"He give me a hundred dollars every month."

"And told you to shut up," I said.

"Didn't have to. Hilly knew, it'd kill him. Hilly drinks some, but he loves me. I been faithful to him forty-three years. I wouldn't never want him to know."

There were tears now in her squinty eyes. Her face was puffy with booze and fat and age and tiredness.

"Did Cheryl Anne know who her father was?" I said.

241

The tears blossomed, and ran down her face. Her heavy shoulders sagged, and her breath began to come hard. She lowered her face suddenly and stared at the ground.

"She did, didn't she?" I said.

Bertha nodded.

"Be hard not to tell her," I said.

"I told her when she a seventeen-year-old girl," Bertha said. "I wanted her to be proud of where she come from. To know that she wasn't just like us."

"And a little after that," I said, "she left town."

"Yes."

"And you didn't hear from her anymore."

Bertha was crying full out now, her head down, her arms at her sides. She shook her head. I didn't have it in me to tell her that her daughter was dead. She'd have to know sometime. But it didn't have to be me who told her.

I put my hand out and patted her shoulder. She pulled away.

"I'm sorry," I said. And turned and got back in my car and drove away.

When I thought about it, on the dark road back to Alton, I figured that she probably sort of knew that her daughter was dead. Which didn't make me feel any better.

41

It was eight-thirty at night and starting to rain when Jefferson let me into the big white house on the rise where Jack Nelson lived. As I stepped into the dim front hall, there was the quiet movement of dogs about me, and the old alpha dog put his nose against the back of my hand.

"Evening, Mr. Spenser," Jefferson said.

"I need to talk to Mr. Nelson," I said. "He in?"

I could hear the smile in Jefferson's voice although the hallway was too dim to see it.

"Mr. Jack always in, sir. What is it you need to see him about?"

"Cheryl Anne Rankin," I said.

We stood silent in the dim, dog-smelling hallway. Jefferson still had a hand on the open door. The old alpha dog sat next to me waiting for me to pat him. I patted him. The silence dragged on. Then Jefferson closed the door softly behind me.

"This way, Mr. Spenser," he said and we went back through the house the same way we had gone last time into the vast glass room where Jack Nelson kept his whiskey.

The last time I'd come, the room had been flooded with light. Now it was dark except for the eccentric glow of the television set. The rain drops flattened against the glass roof, and ran together, and ran off in convoluted streaks. The sound of the rain hitting was a kind of steady rattle in the dark.

Nelson was propped in his chair by the television. The water and the bourbon were at hand. The silent dogs were there. The air-conditioning was still turned up and the chilled room felt like a meat locker.

Nelson looked at me without reaction as I walked toward him. Jefferson held back a little, among the dogs, silent at the periphery.

I said, "Mr. Nelson, remember me?"

Nelson stared at me and shook his head. He seemed to have become more inert since I'd seen him last. Three hundred nearly motionless pounds of booze and suet. The sound was low on the television, where two guys were pretending to wrestle. Nelson's breath wheezed in the quiet room.

"My name is Spenser. I'm a detective from Boston, Mass. I came a while back and talked with you about your daughter."

"No daughter," he rasped.

"I'm sorry, Mr. Nelson, but that's not true. In fact, there's two daughters."

At the dark rim of the glass room Jefferson made a sound like a sigh.

"Nigger lover," Nelson said. He drank some bourbon. His eyes went back to rest on the television set.

"Your daughter Olivia married an African," I said. "Your daughter Cheryl Anne married a rich guy from Boston."

Nelson's eyes never moved from the television. He seemed to settle more deeply into his own mass. The rain streamed off the black glass of the conservatory roof.

"She was murdered a little while ago," I said. "In Boston. I'm trying to find out who."

Nelson drank some more bourbon, and fumbled for the bottle and poured another drink and muddled water into it from the pitcher. While he did this he never took his eyes from the television tube. He spilled some of the bourbon and some of the water. He didn't bother with ice. I stepped in front of the television set.

"You have an illegitimate daughter named Cheryl Anne Rankin," I said.

Nelson bent his head to the side trying to see past me to the screen. I seemed to have no meaning to him. He seemed to know only that I was an object between him and the picture.

"He ain't going to talk, Mr. Spenser," Jefferson said. "He don't talk much anymore."

"Then you'll have to talk, Jefferson," I said. "One way or another, I'm going to find out about Cheryl Anne Rankin. And if that includes getting an extradition warrant on Jumper Jack, then I'll do it."

Jefferson turned a switch somewhere and indirect lighting brightened the room somewhat. Nelson seemed oblivious of it. Jefferson nodded at a couch against the inner wall of the conservatory. We went and sat on it, he at one end, me at the other. Across the room Nelson sat and watched the wrestling match and drank whiskey among his dogs.

"Been with Mr. Jack more than sixty years," Jefferson said. "Fourteen years old, graduate eighth grade, going to be a carpenter."

Jefferson stood suddenly and walked over to the table by Nelson's chair and made himself a drink and one for me and brought them back. He handed me mine and remained standing, holding his in both of his still-strong hands, looking out at the dark rain beyond the conservatory glass.

"Always like tools," he said. "Like to make a miter fit snug. Like things square."

He looked around the conservatory slowly.

"Started working for Mr. Jack's father on this room. Apprentice. But I was good at it, even then, and Mr. Jack's father he say, 'Boy, you a hard worker. Need a boy to work 'round here.' He say, 'You want to work for me?' and I say, 'Sure enough, Mr. Nelson.' And I worked here ever since."

He was looking at the darkness again, and through it probably, back down the corridor of his past.

"Cheryl Anne," I said softly.

"Sure, you right. She Mr. Jack's daughter. Mr. Jack, he a hand with the ladies. And maybe Miss Abby knew it, and maybe she didn't, but nothing come of it, 'cause Mr. Jack, he don't never embarrass her, you understand? He maybe have a fling with a lady, but it always a lady of breeding and position, nobody gonna embarrass Miss Abby."

"Miss Abby was Jack's wife?"

"Yessir."

Jefferson shook his head. Across the room Nelson fumbled together another drink for himself.

"Bertha come here to work in the kitchen. Not a cook, just to peel vegetables, and wash up, that sort of thing. She from Batesburg. She come over on the bus every morning, go home on it every night."

One of the dogs wandered across the room as we talked and jumped up on the couch and turned around three times and lay down between us. Jefferson patted her head absently.

"She don't look like much no more, but she look like something then all right. And she had that thing, you know, Mr. Spenser. She . . . she had a wiggle. She . . . hot, you know?"

"Yeah, I know."

"And Mr. Jack, he can't keep his hands off her."

"It wasn't his hands got him in trouble," I said.

"Yessir. And when she have the baby, Mr. Jack was ashamed. He felt real bad about it and he didn't want Miss Abby to know, and he don't want anyone else to know either. So he give her some money, and he say it is a secret, and long as it stayed a secret, he'd keep giving her the money."

"Hundred bucks a month," I said.

Jefferson shrugged.

"Those times that a lot of money to somebody like Bertha Voss," he said. "And she gets married to Hilly Rankin and she lets him think it's his kid. So it worked out that it stayed secret."

"Except she told her daughter," I said. "And she told her to be proud of who her father was and she told her how rich her father was and the daughter always remembered that, and always hated that he wouldn't acknowledge her, and for reasons that probably have to do with her being crazy, she took the legitimate daughter's name and history."

"Yessir."

"And when she was forty-three years old and broke, she remembered about how rich he was, and she came to him for money."

"Yessir."

The hokum noise of the wrestling match on the television made the silence in the rest of the vast atrium seem somehow more intense. Jefferson went and got two more drinks and brought them back and gave me one. Jumper Jack never stirred. His gaze remained fixed on the television screen.

"Did he pay her?" I said.

"Don't even know who she is," Jefferson said. "Or he says he don't. Hard to say what Mr. Jack know and don't know anymore."

"You pay her?" I said.

"Did for a while. Then no more."

"Why'd you stop?"

Jefferson shook his head softly.

"Ain't no money," he said.

"Jack too?" I said.

"Mr. Jack never had as much as everybody think," Jefferson said. "And he spend what he got."

Jefferson smiled thoughtfully, thinking back over the spending.

"Bought cars and horses, and whiskey and

food and presents for Miss Abby and Miss Livvie, and he spent a lot on women. Mr. Jack always say he didn't waste none. He say he didn't get cheated. Horse players die broke, he say."

"So he's broke?"

"Yessir. This house free and clear, 'bout all."

"What's he use for cash?" I said.

"Don't need much. Feed the dogs, buy whiskey. 'Bout all."

"You get a salary?"

"I still do a little carpentry work, part-time, when Mr. Jack sleeping. My grandson come in, watch him for me. Put in some cabinets for people, do some finish work, that sort of thing. Can't do too much heavy stuff anymore, but I still got the touch for finish."

"You support him," I said.

Jefferson took in some of his drink. I sipped mine. Bourbon wasn't my favorite, but one made do.

"Yessir," Jefferson said.

"And you told Cheryl Anne that there wasn't money to give her."

Jefferson nodded. He was looking out again past the dark fields beyond the atrium. He raised his glass and drank slowly. From the look of the drink it was mostly bourbon, but he drank as if it were milk. The rain washed down along the glass walls of the room.

"And she was unable to hide her disappointment," I said.

"Say she don't believe me," Jefferson said. "Call me a thieving nigger. And she scream at Mr. Jack. He ain't right anymore. You can see that. Anybody see that. Say he her father and he owe her the money. Say he got one week to get her some money. It upset him, her screaming at him like that."

I sipped a little more bourbon. Jefferson finished his and looked at mine. I shook my head. Jefferson went for another and made one too for Jumper Jack. I scratched the hound's ear that lay curled next to me on the couch. I looked at the rain that slid along the curving glass. I looked at Jefferson. He returned the look and we were silent. We both knew. It seemed as if I had known for a long time.

Seeing me scratch the hound's ear, another dog got up and came over and put his head on the edge of the couch. The rest of the dogs noticed this change of position and stood and moved silently around the room, as if ordered by an unseen trainer, and settled back down in realigned order.

"And she left," I said.

Jefferson nodded.

"And went back to Boston."

Nod.

"And you took a framing hammer, with a long handle for leverage, because you're not as strong as you used to be, and you went up there too."

"On the bus," Jefferson said, looking straight at me with no expression I could see. "Three days on the bus."

"And found her address and waited until it was dark and when she walked by you beat her to death."

"Yessir."

Across the room Jumper Jack sat staring at his television, with three dogs in various positions of sleep on the floor around him. He drank half a glass of whiskey as I watched him and dribbled some down his chin and wiped it away with the back of his hand. It was the most active I'd seen him. He never glanced at us. It was as if he were alone in the room with his dogs and his whiskey, except that as I watched, tears rolled slowly down his face.

I put my drink down and rubbed my temples with both hands. The dog whose ear I'd been scratching looked up at me. I scratched his ear again, and he put his head back down on the couch.

"Jefferson," I said, "I'll get back to you."

42

I stood at my stove pouring a thin stream of cornmeal into simmering milk. As it went in, I stirred with a whisk.

"Corn meal mush?" Susan said.

"We gourmets prefer to call it polenta," I said.

I put the whisk down and picked up a wooden spoon and stirred the cornmeal more slowly as it thickened.

"What are those crumby things on the platter?" Susan said.

She was sitting at my counter going through a glass of Gewürztraminer at the speed of erosion. She was wearing a pair of fitted tan slacks, a lemon sweater, and a matching tan coat that was part of the outfit and reached to her knees. She looked like Hollywood's vision of the successful female executive.

"Those are chicken breasts pounded flat and coated with cornbread crumbs," I said. "And flavored with rosemary."

"Will you fry them in lard?" Susan said.

"I will coat a fry pan with corn oil and then pour it out, leaving a thin film in the pan, then I will gently sauté the breast cutlets until golden brown," I said.

"Exactly," Susan said.

"And for dessert," I said, "there's sour cherry pie."

She poured a teaspoon more wine into her glass. Pearl reared up beside her and put her front paws on the counter and made a try for the chicken cutlets. She missed and I picked up a scrap from the cutting board and gave it to her.

"You are rewarding inappropriate behavior," Susan said.

"Yes."

Pearl dashed into the bedroom to eat the chicken scrap. I kept stirring the polenta waiting for it to be right.

"You haven't said a word about things in Alton," Susan said.

"I know. I need to think about it," I said.

"Before you talk to me?" Susan said.

"Yes."

Susan raised her eyebrows and widened her eyes.

"You know," I said, "since I saw you in that guidance office in Smithfield in 1974, I have never looked at you without feeling a small thrill of electricity in my solar plexus."

The polenta was done. I took it off the stove and let it rest on a trivet on the counter.

"Even first thing in the morning when I don't have my face on and I have my hair up?" Susan said.

"Even then," I said. "Although in those circumstances I'm probably reacting to potential."

Susan leaned forward over the counter and kissed me. I kissed her back and felt the residual darkness of that atrium room begin to recede. She pressed her mouth against mine harder as if she could feel my need and put her hands gently on each side of my face and opened her mouth. I put my hands under her arms and lifted her out of the chair and over the counter. It knocked her wine glass over and it broke on the floor. Neither of us paid it any attention. The feel of her against me was rejuvenating, like air long needed, like thirst quenched. We stood for a long time, fiercely together. We never made it to the bedroom. We did well to make the couch.

Afterwards we lay quietly with each other, and Pearl, who had managed to find room on the couch where I would have said there was none.

"In front of the baby," Susan said. Her voice had that quality it always had after love making. As if she were on her way back from somewhere far that she'd been.

"Maybe she showed a little class," I said, "and looked away."

"I seem to recall her barking at a very critical juncture."

"For heaven's sake," I said. "I thought that was you."

Susan giggled into my shoulder where she was resting her head.

"You yanked me right over the counter," she said.

"I didn't yank," I said. "I swept."

"And spilled the wine and broke the wine glass."

"Seemed worth it at the time," I said.

"Usually I like to undress and hang my clothes up neatly."

"So why didn't you resist?" I said.

"And miss all the fun?"

"Of course not."

"When do you think you'll talk about Alton?"

"Pretty soon," I said. "I just have to give it a little time."

Susan nodded and kissed me lightly on the mouth.

"Let's leap up," she said. "And guzzle some polenta."

"Guzzle?"

"Sure."

"We gourmets usually say *savor*," I said.

Susan nodded and got off the couch and got her clothes rearranged. Then she looked at me and smiled and shook her head.

"Right over the goddamned counter," she said.

43

The rain had come up the coast behind me. It had traveled more slowly than I had and arrived in Boston only this morning, when Susan and I, with still the taste of polenta and chicken and Alsatian wine, went to a memorial service for Farrell's lover, whose name had been Brian, in a white Unitarian church in Cambridge. Farrell was there, looking sleepless. And the dead man's parents were there. The mother, stiff with tranquilizers and pale with grief, leaned heavily on her husband, a burly man with a large gray moustache. He looked puzzled, as much as anything, as he held his wife up.

Susan and I sat near the back of the small plain church, while the minister blathered. It was probably not his fault that he blathered. Ministers are expected to speak as if death were not the final emperor. But it came out, as it usually did, blather. Farrell sat with a guy that looked like him, and a woman and two small children. Brian's mother and father sat across the aisle.

There were maybe eight other people in the

church. I didn't recognize any of them except Quirk, who stood in the back, his hands folded calmly in front of him, his face without expression. The church doors stood open and the gray rain came bleakly down on the black street. Susan held my hand.

After the service, Farrell came out of the church and introduced us to the guy that looked like him. It was his brother. The woman was his brother's wife, and the kids were Farrell's nephews.

"My mother and father wouldn't come," he said.

"How too bad for them," Susan said.

Quirk came to stand beside us.

"Thank you for coming, Lieutenant," Farrell said.

"Sure," Quirk said.

Farrell moved on with his brother on one side and his sister-in-law on the other. His nephews, small and quiet, frightened by death, probably, each held a parental hand.

"Tough," Quirk said. "You back from another visit to South Carolina?"

We were standing under an overhang out of the cold rain, which came grimly down.

"Yeah."

"You got anything?"

"I don't know yet."

Quirk frowned.

"What the hell does that mean?" he said.

"Means I don't know yet."

Quirk looked at Susan. She smiled like Mona Lisa.

"Christ," Quirk said to her. "You get better every time I see you."

"Thank you, Martin," she said.

He looked back at me.

"Call me when you know," he said, and turned his raincoat collar up and went down the steps to an unmarked police car and drove away. I turned up my collar too, and took Susan's hand, and walked down the steps and away from the church in the rain, which was cold and hard and without respite.

44

The morning was overcast, and hard-looking. I was in my office, thinking about Jefferson, and feeling like Hamlet, but older, when Farrell came in carrying two coffees in a white paper bag. He took them out, handed me one, and sat down.

"It bother you that Stratton was so interested in this case?" he said.

"He wants to be President," I said.

"And all he was trying to cover up was adultery?"

I shrugged.

"The cover-up was more dangerous to him than what he was trying to cover up," Farrell said.

"Guys like Stratton don't think that way. They think about fixing, about putting a new spin on it, about reorganizing it so it comes out their way."

"He stole most of the Tripps' money," Farrell said.

I sat back in my chair.

"Why do you know that and I don't?" I said.

Farrell was carefully prying the plastic cap off his paper coffee cup, holding it away from him so it wouldn't spill on him. He got the cover off and blew on the coffee gently for a moment, and then took a swallow. His face was still tight with grief, but there was also a hint of self-satisfaction.

"You been thinking about who killed the woman," Farrell said. "I been thinking about other stuff — like Stratton, like what the hell happened to all that money. Everybody says Mrs. Tripp spent it all, but on what? It's hard to go through that kind of money at Bloomingdale's."

"So you chased Tripp's expenditures," I said.

"Yeah. Checks written by him, or her. They had a joint account. His didn't show us anything unusual. He kept writing them even when there was no money. But you already knew that."

"Mine bounced," I said.

"There's a clue," Farrell said. He drank some more coffee. "Her checks were more interesting."

"I didn't see any of hers when I looked at his checkbook," I said. "But she'd been dead awhile, probably hadn't written any."

"Good point," Farrell said. "I went back about five years."

"Tripp didn't object?"

Farrell shook his head. "Didn't talk to him," he said. "I went through the bank's records. She wrote regular, like monthly, large checks to an organization called The Better Government Coalition, which is located in a post office box in Cambridge, and headed by a guy named Windsor Freedman. We're having a little trouble locating Windsor. He lists his address as University Green on Mt. Auburn Street. It's a condo complex, and nobody there ever heard of him. But the Mass. Secretary of State's office lists The Better Government Coalition as a subsidiary of The American Democratic Imperative in D.C. And the president of that operation is a guy named Mal Chapin."

Farrell paused to drink coffee. He looked at me while he swallowed.

"I know that name," I said.

"So did Quirk," Farrell said. "You remember where you heard it?"

"Motel room in Alton, South Carolina," I said. "Mal Chapin is in Stratton's office."

"Pretty good," Farrell said. "Of course I mentioned that Quirk knew it too; that was a clue."

"Yeah," I said. "I'm excited. Usually when I get a clue, I trip over it, and skin my knee."

"Quirk's talking with somebody in the FBI,

see about getting one of their accountants to check out The Democratic Imperative, see what they do with their money."

"You figure it supports Stratton."

"Sure," Farrell said. "A charity with no offices, wholly owned by another charity, with no offices, headed by a guy works for Stratton. What do you think we'll find out?"

"That it supports Stratton," I said.

"That's what we'll find out," Farrell said. "Maybe there's a motive in it. Maybe Olivia Nelson knew what was going on and they had a lover's quarrel and she was going to blow the whistle on him."

"And he got a hammer and beat her brains out one night?"

"Maybe he had it done."

"By somebody that would use a hammer?"

"Possible."

"Sure," I said. "But likely?"

Farrell shook his head slowly.

"Not likely."

"Stratton know you've been investigating him?"

"Shouldn't," Farrell said.

"I'd like to bring them all together and confront him with it."

"All of who?"

"Tripp, his kids, Stratton, see what comes out of it."

Farrell stared at me for a couple of long moments. Then he shook his head slowly.

"You're still trying to fix that family," Farrell said. "You just want to shake the old man out of his trance if you can."

I shrugged, drank some coffee.

"You could just stick to finding out who killed the woman?"

"Might make sense to bring them together," I said. "Something might pop out. No harm to it."

"No harm to you," he said. "Might be some harm to a detective second grade who accuses a U. S. Senator of a felony without all his evidence in yet."

I nodded.

"Be stupid to do that," Farrell said. "Especially if being a gay detective second grade made command staff ill at ease anyway, so to speak."

I nodded again.

"Unless, of course, you made the charge," Farrell said.

"Without saying how I knew it," I said. "And you simply called us together to give the Senator a chance to respond privately, before any formal inquiry began."

"A chance to lay these baseless charges to rest," Farrell said.

"Sure," I said.

"Want to meet here?"

"I'm the guy making the baseless charges," I said.

"Okay," Farrell said.

There was silence while we both drank the rest of our coffee. Then Farrell put his cup in my wastebasket and stood.

"I'll be in touch," he said.

"I know you are going out a little ways on a limb," I said. "Thanks."

"Nice of you to come to the funeral," Farrell said.

45

They came. Nobody seemed very pleased about it, but Farrell got them there. The three Tripps came together, and Stratton came with two guys in London Fog raincoats who waited in the corridor outside my office, and looked intrepid.

Stratton looked at neither Farrell, nor at me. He shook hands with Loudon Tripp and put a hand on his shoulder while he did it. Unspoken condolence. Then Stratton shook Chip's hand and they gave each other a manly hug and clap on the back.

"Great to see you, Bob," Chip said. He wasn't very old and you could tell he liked calling a U. S. Senator by his first name.

We got arranged. Stratton and Loudon Tripp in the two client chairs. Farrell leaning on the wall to my left. The two Tripp children to my right, a little back from the group. Chip looking aggressive, ready to slap a half nelson on someone, Meredith looking passively at the floor.

"Okay, gentlemen," Stratton said. He smiled at Meredith, who made no eye contact. "And lady. Let's get to it. You called us together, Officer. What have you got?"

Stratton looked tanned and healthy. His hair was perfectly trimmed and trying its best to look plentiful. His pinstripe suit was well cut. His white shirt crisp and new. He still wore his trench coat, unbuttoned, the belt tucked into the pockets. All in all he was direct, competent, square dealing, straight shooting, judicious, and nice.

Farrell looked edgy and tired.

"Spenser here came to me with some allegations which I thought we'd best confront privately, Senator."

Stratton's glance shifted to me. The pale blue eyes as hard as chrome.

"Allegations?"

"Involving the Tripps," Farrell said.

Stratton continued to stare at me.

"You are becoming something of a pain in the butt," he said. "Maybe I should have put you out of business a while ago."

"Being a pain in the butt is my profession," I said. "What's the first word that comes to mind when I say The Better Government Coalition?"

Stratton's eyes became more opaque.

"The American Democratic Imperative?" I said.

Stratton didn't speak.

"Mal Chapin?"

Stratton stood up.

"That is just about enough of that," he said. "I am not going to sit here and listen to some cheap private eye trolling for some way to make a name for himself at my expense."

"I'm cheaper than you think," I said. "The only check I got for this job bounced."

Stratton turned toward the door. Farrell went and leaned against it.

"Why not hear him out, Senator, in front of witnesses. Maybe he'll do something actionable."

"You get out of my way," Stratton said.

Farrell's voice was soft. He was standing face to face with Stratton.

"Sit down," he said.

"Who in hell do you think . . . ?" Stratton started.

"Now."

Stratton stepped back from the force of the single word.

"I'm sick of you, Stratton," Farrell said. "I'm sick of the phony macho. I'm sick of the self-importance. I'm sick of the way you comb your hair over your goddamned bald spot. Sit and listen or I'll bust your stupid senatorial ass."

"What charge?" Stratton said. But it was weak. The game was over the moment Stratton stepped back.

"Violation of no-dork zoning regulations,"

Farrell said. "Sit down."

Stratton sat.

"What's the first word that comes to mind," I said, "when I say The Better Government Coalition? The American Democratic Imperative? Mal Chapin?"

"Mal works for me," Stratton said. His voice shook a little. "In my office. I don't know those other things."

"Mal work for you full-time?" I said.

"Yes. He's my chief of staff."

"Hard job?"

"Hard." Stratton began to make a come back. He was on familiar ground. "And thankless. We are involved in very many crucial national and international issues. Mal works ten, fifteen hours a day."

"Not much time for another job," I said.

Stratton realized he'd been led down the path. He tried to backtrack.

"Certainly he works hard, but what he does in his off hours . . ." Stratton shrugged and spread his hands.

"He's listed as the President of The American Democratic Imperative," I said. "A charitable organization based in Washington."

Stratton shook his head in silence.

"Before her death, Olivia Nelson regularly made large contributions to The Better Government Coalition, in Cambridge. The Better

Government Coalition is listed as a subsidiary of the American Democratic Imperative, which is headed by your chief of staff."

Stratton stared straight ahead.

"And you have told me directly that you were intimate with Olivia Nelson," I said.

The words hung in the room, drifting like the dust of ruination.

Then Loudon Tripp said, "Enough. I'll hear no more, Spenser. I'm responsible for all of this. I hired you. I brought you and your dirty mind and your gutter morals into all of this. And now you contrive to dirty my dead wife and my friend with one lie."

"He's not your friend, Mr. Tripp," I said. "He slept with your wife. He stole your money."

"No," Tripp said. "I'll hear no more."

He stood up. Chip stepped in beside him.

"You can't stop me," he said to Farrell. "Come on, kids."

"Last chance," I said to Tripp. "For all of you. You've got to look at this. You've got to stop pretending."

"Get out of my way," Tripp said again. His voice sounded strangled. "Not my wife, not with my friend."

He moved past Farrell toward the door. Chip went with him, knotted with excitement, frantic to explode. Meredith stared at him

271

with her mouth half open, motionless.

"Come along, Meredith," Tripp said. Except that his voice was strangled, he spoke to her as if she were dawdling by a toy store.

"He's . . . not . . . your . . . friend," Meredith said.

"Meredith," Tripp said. The squeezed-out voice was parental — exasperated, long-suffering — but not unloving.

"For crissake, Mere," Chip said.

"He . . . *was* . . . fucking her," Meredith said.

Tripp flinched. Chip's face reddened.

"He was fucking me," she said in a rush. "Since I was fourteen and he came in my room at one of those big parties."

The silence in the room was stifling. No one moved. Meredith was rigid, her hands at her sides, a look of shock on her face.

"Jesus," Chip said. "Mere, why didn't you . . . ?"

"Dr. Faye says I was getting even with Mommy, and I wanted Daddy to . . ." She put both her hands suddenly over her mouth and pressed them, palm open, hard against her face, and slowly slid her back down the wall until she was sitting on the floor, her legs splayed in front of her. Chip looked at his father, who seemed frozen in time, then he went suddenly to his knees beside his sister and put his arms around her and pressed her head against his chest. She let him hold her there.

Loudon Tripp stared for a moment at both of them, and then, without looking at anyone else, he walked across my office and out the door and down the corridor past the two guys in their London Fogs. They looked in the office uncertainly. Farrell shook his head at them and they stepped away from the door. Stratton continued to sit in his chair with his head down, staring at the floor, contemplating his ruin.

Human voices wake us, and we drown.

46

On a bright Sunday morning, Susan and I took Pearl over to Harvard Stadium to let her run. We sat in the first row of the stands while Pearl coursed the football field alert for game birds, or Twinkie wrappers. Her nose was down, her tail was up, and her whole self seemed attenuated, as she raced back and forth over the field where generations of young Harvard men had so fiercely fought.

"Your name was in the paper this morning," Susan said. She was wearing a black and lavender warm-up suit, and her dark hair shone in the sunshine.

"Did you cut it out and put it up on the refrigerator with a little magnet?"

"Most of the story was the Senator Stratton indictment. Detective Farrell is quoted extensively."

Pearl spotted a covey of pigeons near the thirty-yard line and went into her low stalk. The closer she got, the slower she went, until finally the pigeons flew up and Pearl dashed to where they had been and wagged her tail.

"He did the work," I said. "And he did

it even though he wasn't feeling too swell."

"How are you feeling?" Susan said. "You did some work too."

"Not enough," I said.

"You're worrying about the Tripps," Susan said.

"Wouldn't you?" I said.

"Up to a point," Susan said. "You didn't get them into this dysfunctional mess. You have done something to start getting them out of it."

"By pulling the lid off," I said.

Susan nodded. "By pulling the lid off. Someone had to. If it could have happened more gently, and more gradually, that would have been better. But you didn't control that."

I nodded.

Pearl finished hunting the stadium, and came up into the stands, and sat in front of us with her mouth open and her tongue hanging out.

"Dr. Faye is a well-respected and experienced therapist," Susan said.

I nodded again. We were near the open end of the stadium. Across Soldiers Field Road, the river moved its oblivious way toward Boston Harbor.

Susan put her cheek against my shoulder.

"And," she said, "you're kind of cute."

"There's consolation in that," I said.

I put Pearl's leash on, and we stood and started out of the stands. Susan took my hand and we strolled back through the Harvard Athletic Complex toward the Larz Anderson Bridge. There was a red light at the pedestrian crossing. We stopped.

"What are you going to do about the murder?" Susan said.

"When Jefferson told me the truth that night," I said, "there were six or eight dogs sleeping in the atrium."

The light changed and we started across.

"I think I'll let them lie."

The employees of THORNDIKE PRESS hope you have enjoyed this Large Print book. All our Large Print books are designed for easy reading — and they're made to last.

Other Thorndike Large Print books are available at your library, through selected bookstores, or directly from us. Suggestions for books you would like to see in Large Print are always welcome.

For more information about current and upcoming titles, please call or mail your name and address to:

THORNDIKE PRESS
PO Box 159
Thorndike, Maine 04986
800/223-6121
207/948-2962